Around t...

Pack your bags and leave the postfestivity blues behind! This January, Harlequin Romance presents a whirlwind tour to some stunning international locations—and we want you to join us. Whether you're looking for sun, sea or snow, we've got you covered. So let yourself be swept away by these beautiful romances and discover how four couples make it to their true destination... happy-ever-after!

Get ready for the trip of a lifetime with...

Their Hawaiian Marriage Reunion
by Cara Colter

Copenhagen Escape with the Billionaire
by Sophie Pembroke

Prince's Proposal for the Canadian Cameras
by Nina Singh

Cinderella's Moroccan Midnight Kiss
by Nina Milne

All available now!

COPENHAGEN ESCAPE WITH THE BILLIONAIRE

SOPHIE PEMBROKE

Harlequin

ROMANCE

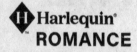

ROMANCE

ISBN-13: 978-1-335-21626-7

Copenhagen Escape with the Billionaire

Harlequin Enterprises ULC
22 Adelaide St. West, 41st Floor
Toronto, Ontario M5H 4E3, Canada
www.Harlequin.com

Printed in U.S.A.

Sophie Pembroke has been dreaming, reading and writing romance ever since she read her first Harlequin novel as part of her English literature degree at Lancaster University, so getting to write romantic fiction for a living really is a dream come true! Born in Abu Dhabi, Sophie grew up in Wales and now lives in a little Hertfordshire market town with her scientist husband, her incredibly imaginative and creative daughter, and her adventurous, adorable little boy. In Sophie's world, happy *is* forever after, everything stops for tea and there's always time for one more page...

Books by Sophie Pembroke

Harlequin Romance

Blame It on the Mistletoe

Christmas Bride's Stand-In Groom

Dream Destinations

Their Icelandic Marriage Reunion
Baby Surprise in Costa Rica

The Heirs of Wishcliffe

Vegas Wedding to Forever
Their Second Chance Miracle
Baby on the Rebel Heir's Doorstep

Twin Sister Swap

Cinderella in the Spotlight
Socialite's Nine-Month Secret

The Princess and the Rebel Billionaire
Best Man with Benefits

Visit the Author Profile page
at Harlequin.com for more titles.

For Laurie, for everything

Praise for
Sophie Pembroke

CHAPTER ONE

Ellie Peters tucked her hair behind her ears, pushed her glasses up her nose, straightened her spine and…reached for her cup of tea, instead of focusing on the screen in front of her. The accusatory *blank* screen. The one that should have been filled with chapters and chapters of witty, wise and warm observations on happiness by now—but wasn't.

Oh, she'd started the book. She'd written a whole proposal and sample chapters for her editor before they'd paid her the advance that made the whole thing possible. There was a detailed outline, plans and joyous suggestions for research trips and adventures, seeking out happiness here in Denmark, one of the happiest countries in the world. And normally that would be enough to ensure the work got done. When Ellie committed to doing something— for someone else, at least—it got done, no ifs or buts. Keeping that kind of commitment to things she promised *herself* was a little more hit and miss. But she prided herself on being someone that others could rely on to keep her word. She'd said she'd write a book on happiness, so she would write a book on happiness.

The only problem was, she'd written that book proposal back when she *was* happy. When her marriage seemed solid, her day-to-day work as a features editor for a glossy women's magazine proving both fun and satisfactorily lucrative. When her London townhouse felt like home, and she had friends and family she could rely on. When a research trip to Denmark—where, not coincidentally, her best friend Lily had moved after marrying her Viking true love, Anders—seemed like an adventure. A chance to make her life even more fulfilling, happy and enviable.

Now? Now things were different.

Now, Denmark was an escape. As evidenced by the fact that it was New Year's Eve in Copenhagen and she was sitting in semi-darkness, one solitary candle—a present from Lily—burning beside her on the desk, staring at a still blank page.

She'd escaped her life by running away to spend four whole months searching for happiness hacks in Denmark. But she couldn't escape her deadline.

And Ellie just would not let down her editor, or her readers. Especially not when she was already letting down her mother and her half-sister, for perhaps the first time in her life.

Who even am I, these days?

Ellie wasn't sure she recognised herself any longer. And she knew her family were baffled by her sudden inability to go along with everything they asked of her.

Maybe if I'd ever said no to them before, this wouldn't be such a shock. Or if I'd ever admitted to being anything other than happy about how my life has turned out.

With a sigh, she clicked out of the empty document and back onto her web browser. Immediately, her own face—beaming, happy—filled square after square of the screen. Photos of her in London, arms around friends or dressed to the nines. Photos of her boarding her plane to Denmark, passport in hand, looking excited and only a little nervous. Selfies from around Copenhagen, filtered to look brighter and happier than the Danish city ever could in winter.

All of them a tiny fake moment in time, captured for observers rather than herself.

Ellie had built up quite a following online—

first as someone 'in the know' in London, and now as a happiness adventurer or influencer abroad. Her publisher was thrilled she had so much interaction from her fans. Which was fine for her publisher—nobody there had to keep up with answering all the messages and comments in her peppiest, happiest tone.

Checking her notifications, she sent fast, emoji-heavy replies to some of her most faithful followers.

One of them read:

So exciting to see you growing out your natural grey hair! I grew mine out two years ago and haven't looked back!

Ellie winced. There was no way she could admit that the grey regrowth since her last colour and cut was due to her not having the courage to find a Danish hairdresser that could replicate it—even though Lily had recommended hers. She'd looked at the box dyes on the shelf, but hadn't trusted herself either. What if the instructions were only in Danish? Besides, she'd been wearing a woolly hat pretty much permanently since she arrived, so it wasn't as if her roots were often on display.

After a moment's thought, she replied.

I'm learning that happiness requires authenticity. I'm forty-four—I have some grey hairs. That's who I am and I'm happy with it!

That sounded on brand, right? And freed her from having to find a hairdresser before she headed back to London in another six weeks. Although she might have to see it through, now she'd commented about authenticity. Would it be inauthentic to dye it again now? Probably. Maybe there was some sort of blended look she could get her regular hairdresser to implement—half highlights, half grey or something. She should research that.

Before she could open the search browser though, she shut herself down. No distractions. She was supposed to be *working*. Deadline, remember?

Ellie clicked back to the blank document again. She couldn't face being the sort of authentic her followers expected from her right now—which was, of course, about as inauthentic as it got.

Her phone buzzed and she picked it up, pretending to herself that she wasn't eager for the distraction. It could be important, right?

Hey, El! Getting this message in now in case the lines are jammed at midnight. Just wanted to say how proud I am of my little sis and this huge adventure you're on. You haven't let the world get you down, even when nobody would have blamed you for it. It makes me so happy to see how well you're doing over there in Denmark! Can't wait to hear all about it properly when you're back home at the end of Feb. Until then, stay happy, keep having fun...and find a hot guy to kiss at midnight for me! Sarah xxx

Ellie's jaw tightened as she read through the message from her older sister. At least this sojourn in Denmark was making *somebody* happy. If even Sarah, who knew everything, believed she'd genuinely come here for work and self-growth, rather than to run away from everything she'd left behind in Britain, she had to be doing something right.

Her phone buzzed again—another message from Sarah.

I know, I know, you're not going to rely on a man for happiness ever again. Just have fun though, yeah?!

Well, that much was true, at least. Ellie was *definitely* never finding her happiness in a guy again. She'd learned that lesson too well from her now ex-husband.

Ellie's gaze flicked up towards the clock. The afternoon had disappeared without her noticing. It was hard, sometimes, to tell the passing of time when there was so little daylight to judge it by. In Copenhagen in December, the sun didn't rise until long after breakfast, and it was down again by mid-afternoon. Lily claimed that the day wasn't *much* shorter than it would be in London at this time of year, being on a similar latitude, but it still *felt* it.

Just one reason that Ellie was glad Lily had moved to Denmark rather than, say, Northern Finland. The Finns might have claimed the happiest country crown recently, but with less than three hours of daylight in December, Ellie wasn't sure she could have faked happiness there if she'd tried.

And Copenhagen *was* lovely. She'd explored a lot of it on foot, alone, and found it charming. She just wasn't sure what there was about the place to make the Danes so much *happier* than other nations. And at this point, halfway through her Danish stay, she wasn't sure she was ever going to figure it out. She'd read all the studies and the articles about work-life balance, family support and high taxes providing high levels of care. She just couldn't quite see what that had to offer *her*—a self-employed, newly single woman who was child-free by choice.

She sighed, and pushed her desk chair away from her computer. If anyone was going to teach her about happiness in Denmark, it would surely be the sickeningly loved up newlyweds, Lily and Anders. They'd invited her to spend New Year's Eve with them and a few friends, and Ellie hadn't been able to find a polite way to refuse. Plus, she was hoping that those Danish friends might have some happiness insights that would kickstart her book writing. Besides, there was no way Lily was going to allow her to 'stay in her little rented flat and moulder away as the clock ticked midnight'—to quote Lily herself.

So Ellie would go and see in the new year with her friends—which, honestly, was about as close to true happiness as she could imagine getting here in Copenhagen.

But what did she know? Maybe tonight would be the night that the secrets to happiness revealed themselves to her.

As long as they didn't come attached to a man, she'd welcome them in.

Jesper Mikkelsen drummed his fingertips along the arm of the perfectly designed visitor's chair in his brother-in-law's office. Or ex-brother-in-law, he supposed. Did a man lose his relatives by marriage after the death of his wife? Jesper wasn't sure. Maybe he'd ask Will.

Or maybe not. His sister's death was still a painful open wound for both of them. No need to bring it up tonight, when the new year beckoned, full of promise.

Besides, Will would still be his financial advisor, even if he wasn't technically a brother any more. That was something. Maybe he'd even still be a friend.

Jesper had lost a lot of people over the last few years. Most of them, he was fine without. But he'd hate to lose Will, too.

He gazed around the empty office, taking in all the touches that made it special. The beautiful Danish furniture—all costing a fortune, but worth every krone, in Jesper's opinion. The building deserved it—the way it caught the last of the disappearing daylight, but at an angle that didn't blind him, the graceful lines of the exterior that always felt as if they were welcoming him in. Yes, Will had done well with this office.

But eventually, Jesper had to look at the desk. There wasn't much on it: Will's laptop, a small potted plant and a single photo frame containing the last photo ever taken of the three of them together—Jesper, Will and Agnes.

She was pregnant when that was taken, Jesper realised with a start. *Did she know it?*

He hadn't. He hadn't known until the doctor at the American hospital where she succumbed to her injuries after the car crash let it slip. If she had known, she hadn't told him. But then, she hadn't told him much of anything, towards the end.

Jesper shook the thought away and got to his feet, pacing towards the window even as the office door opened and Will reappeared.

'Sorry about that,' he said with a smile. 'Just something I wanted to get tidied up before the holiday.' New Year's Eve wasn't a public holiday, but New Year's Day was. Jesper wondered how many people in Will's office were actually working today, and how many had taken it off to prepare for the celebrating ahead. At the least, most of them would have finished early—or earlier than Jesper was used to after years running his own business in America.

Another new year to enjoy. Sometimes it still seemed impossible that the world kept spinning.

'I'm surprised you were even in the office today,' Jesper said as Will took his seat behind his desk. 'Don't you and Matthew have your usual New Year's Eve dinner party tonight?'

'We do—as you'd know if you'd let us invite you.' Will gave him a stern look. 'You know, I was really hoping that now you're back from the wilderness and around people again, you might be ready to, well, actually be around people again.'

'I am!' Jesper protested. 'Many people. Well, some.' More than he had been in the years immediately following Agnes's death, anyway. The years he'd spent avoiding society, after his move back from the States, when he'd been trying to find a new way to exist in a world he barely recognised.

He'd done it, though. Those wilderness years, as Will called them, had saved him, in lots of ways.

It was just learning to live in the regular world again that was hard.

'So, what are you doing this New Year's Eve?' Will rested his forearms on the desk and leaned towards him. 'Other than deciding to hold this meeting to check on your financial health and wellbeing—a meeting which, I feel, really could have waited until after the holiday.'

'I just asked if you were in!' Jesper protested. 'You were working anyway. Don't blame me for that. And, actually, I only asked because I needed to be in Copenhagen today anyway—because I have New Year plans.'

Will raised his eyebrows. '*Actual* plans, or moping alone watching other peoples' fireworks from a hotel room plans? Because I can still call home and have Matthew set an extra place for dinner...'

'As lovely as that would be, I really do have plans.' It wasn't that Jesper didn't want to spend the evening with his ex-brother-in-law and his husband, it was just that... Will and Matthew's New Year's Eve dinners were legendary. The sort of event that took much longer than the single public holiday that followed to recover from. And Jesper didn't do that sort of extreme any more.

Time was, he'd have worked all day on the thirty-first of December, cramming as many last-minute meetings and actions as possible into the old year, before changing into his tuxedo, grabbing a car to pick up Agnes, who would be stunning in something expensive and revealing, but probably mad at him for being late, then heading out across Manhattan to at least one but often more parties that they just had to be seen at.

If they'd been home in Denmark for the holidays, he'd still have worked—just in the hotel suite they'd have booked, instead of his own office. Then they'd have made their way to Will and Matthew's for the party of the year. They'd eat and drink and laugh and talk all night, before heading up to their roof garden to watch the fireworks from across the city.

And he'd have been back at his desk by seven the next morning, hangover and holiday be-damned. That was the sort of life he'd lived, for too long.

'Really?' Will looked pleasantly surprised at the idea that Jesper really was re-entering society. 'What plans?'

'My friend Anders and his wife Lily have invited me to join them for a low-key supper,' Jesper said. 'Just a few friends, apparently. Nothing too overwhelming. Then a trip to the Tivoli Gardens for midnight itself.' Which probably would be overwhelming in a 'lots of people' way, but at least not a 'lots of people he had to talk to' way. At least at Lily and Anders' cosy flat he could fade into the background in a small group.

'A few friends?' Will smirked. 'Sounds like they're setting you up with someone. That's exactly what Matthew says when he wants to introduce a couple he thinks will hit it off without letting on that's what he's doing.'

'Anders wouldn't do that.' Jesper was almost certain about that. Lily, however... Anders *had* mentioned something about a friend of Lily's visiting from London last time they'd talked. Would that friend be there too, or had they gone home already? At least there would be other people around as a buffer.

'Well, we'll see,' Will said with a smirk. 'Maybe it would do you good to meet someone to kiss at midnight. Part of rejoining the real world.'

Jesper shot him a look. 'I'd have thought you, of all people, wouldn't be encouraging me to get out there and fall in love again.'

Will's smile turned slightly pitying. 'It's been three years since Agnes...left us. You don't have to live in perpetual mourning your whole life, you know. You still get to live.'

Jesper wasn't really all so sure about that. The mistakes he'd made... He wasn't sure he deserved that kind of happiness. Love was too much of a risk.

'And kissing some random woman at midnight isn't the same as falling in love, anyway,' Will went on. 'It doesn't have to be all or nothing, Jes. It can just be fun. A moment of happiness. You deserve that.'

'I am happy,' Jesper said automatically. He'd spent nearly three years, mostly alone in the wilderness, finding that even keel of existence that brought him out of the pit of grief and guilt after Agnes' death and back up to the contentment he now enjoyed. He was happy. He'd fought hard for it.

'Are you?' Will asked softly. 'I hope so. I really do.'

Lily and Anders' flat was everything Ellie had imagined a Danish home would be, before she came to Copenhagen. Beautiful Scandi design, zero clutter but perfectly placed cosy touches everywhere—candles that gave the space a warm glow, knitted and fluffy throw blankets for when the night grew cool, and everything in calming tones of neutral colours.

Ellie loved it, but it was basically the exact opposite of anywhere she had ever lived before.

'It's all about the hygge,' Lily had told her, the first time she'd visited. 'It's cold here in the winter, and dark. People spend a lot of time in their houses, so they want them to be warm, comforting places to be.'

Settled on Lily's white couch with a glass

of white wine on New Year's Eve, Ellie had to admit, it did feel comforting, and comfortable. At least here she was with friends—people who knew her, understood her and what she'd been through, and loved her all the same. She didn't have to put on a facade of happiness for Lily, and she'd never appreciated that as much as she did right now.

Until she asked, 'When is everyone else getting here?' and Anders replied, 'Well, Jesper should be here soon. He had a meeting, but he promised he wouldn't be late.'

Ellie's whole body stiffened, and she even pulled back from reaching for one of the delicious delicacies on the charcuterie plate Lily had set out on the wooden tray that topped the cushioned surface of the multi-purpose foot rest and coffee table. 'Jesper? Just Jesper? I thought…'

She'd thought there'd be a group of them. Now she was starting to sniff a set-up.

'Oh, well, we invited a whole gang, of course, but sadly no one else could make it.' Lily's breezy excuses were completely unconvincing to anyone who'd known her as long as Ellie had—and that was before she spotted Anders looking utterly baffled by his wife's statement.

'We did?' he asked. 'I thought the idea was—'

He broke off as Lily elbowed him in the ribs on her way past.

Definitely a set-up. Ellie sighed. She should have guessed.

But it was too late to back out now. She'd just have to make the best of it.

'So, who is Jesper?' Maybe he'd be good for Danish happiness research, anyway—although she was certain that wasn't what Lily had in mind.

'He's an old friend of Anders',' Lily explained. 'He happens to be in the city for the weekend and, well, it's been a while since we saw him, so we thought it would be nice to invite him along tonight. You'll like him!'

Ellie gave her oldest friend a look that said very clearly that she knew exactly what Lily was doing and she did not approve. Lily winced and looked away. Oh, this was going to be a disaster. No amount of book research was worth an unexpected blind date on New Year's Eve. What if it was an utter disaster and set the tone for the whole year ahead? Okay, that was probably taking superstition too far, but really, given everything that had happened in her life lately, Ellie wasn't taking any chances.

Before she could come up with any even half convincing excuses to leave, there was a knock at the door and Lily skipped away to answer it. Ellie sat, tensed on the sofa, waiting to see what this Jesper looked like. She'd met a few of Anders's friends already, and they all looked a lot like him—big and blond and Viking-like. She imagined Jesper would be the same.

But the man who handed Lily a small potted plant and a bottle of red wine wasn't much like Anders at all. He was dark where Anders was fair, although his hair was greying significantly at the temples and there was white in his short beard, too. He had lines around his eyes that creased up when he smiled at the joke Anders made—in Danish, and too fast for Ellie to try and translate, so presumably not for her ears. His eyes were a bright, sharp blue that she could distinguish even from across the room, which made her strangely uncomfortable. Still, she got to her feet and smoothed down the wool of her knit skirt over her thermal tights—too hot for the flat, but she'd need them later, Lily had assured her.

'Jesper, this is Lily's friend Ellie, from London,' Anders said, gesturing towards her. 'And Ellie, this is one of my very oldest friends, Jesper.'

'It's a pleasure to meet you.' Jesper stepped towards her with a warm smile and an outstretched hand. His voice was lower than she'd expected, the rumbling, gravelly sort of voice that she could feel in her chest. It unsettled her almost as much as his eyes which, up close, were even more striking. Worse, she couldn't shake the feeling that he saw far deeper than most people—into the heart of her. Somehow, she sensed that this man wouldn't buy the fake versions of happiness she'd been peddling online.

'And you.' Her throat felt scratchy as she spoke, and she swallowed as she took his hand, looking up into those too blue eyes. Her palm brushed against his and she felt honest-to-God sparks flash between them.

Probably the thermal tights. Static electricity, that's all.

Except it wasn't. And if the slightly stunned look in Jesper's eyes was anything to go by, she wasn't the only one feeling it.

Ellie wasn't sure what unsettled her most. The fact that he was gorgeous and made her skin spark when she touched him, or the way that she knew, without quite knowing how, that this man would see the real her, far more than anyone else did, if she let him.

She'd just have to make sure she didn't let him, then.

Ellie dropped his hand and stepped away again, reaching for her wine.

'Jesper was living in the States until a few years ago,' Lily said, obviously keen to make conversation and find common ground—and perhaps convince Ellie that her obvious set-up wasn't a terrible, impulsive idea. 'New York. You lived there once, too, didn't you, Ellie?'

'I did.' It had been just after they were married, and she and Dave had still been madly in love. When his job offered a secondment to the Big Apple for two years, they'd jumped at it. It had been an adventure—a real one, not like this manufactured one she was currently undertaking. Every day had brought new experiences, new discoveries about the city around them—and about each other. It was hard to remember being that young, that happy, that optimistic, now. 'It was a long time ago.'

'And now you are in Denmark.' Jesper's voice held traces of American and Danish accents, mingled together—although his English was clearly perfect. And it would have been a damn sight better than her Danish even if it hadn't been. And his voice… Ellie forced herself to ignore the way it seemed to vibrate inside her chest when he spoke and concentrated on what he was saying. 'What brings you here now?'

'Ellie is researching why we Danes are so happy!' Anders answered for her before Ellie could even open her mouth. 'I told her, it is because we are lucky enough to be born Danish, in this magical part of the world, but apparently that's not enough to write a book about.'

'I see.' There was something of a shadow behind Jesper's eyes as he answered, and Ellie got the strange impression that he *did* see. That he understood something of a desperate search for happiness in the face of unsurmountable odds. It made her want to know him better, which was annoying. She hated it when Lily was right about these things. 'And have you had much luck? Have many of my other countrymen and women been able to share better insights than our friend Anders, here?'

Ellie glanced away, towards the darkened windows. Lily hadn't pulled the shades yet, and outside the night seemed to press in, smothering them.

'To be honest, it has been difficult to find many people to talk to about it,' she admitted. 'The city is busy, but even in the after-work hours most of the people I find to talk to are tourists.' She didn't add that she hadn't tried *very* hard. A few half-hearted attempts in the cafés had sapped her hope of the answer to true happiness falling into her lap, and after that she'd sort of lost the energy to keep looking.

'It is the wrong time of year,' Jesper said knowledgeably—even though Ellie had no earthly idea what he meant.

'That's what I said!' Anders pointed a finger at Lily. 'And you told me not to get involved.' Lily rolled her eyes.

'The wrong time of year how, exactly?' Ellie asked.

'In the winter, we Danes tend to hunker down—to embrace the hygge,' Jesper explained. He'd sat down on the sofa beside her, and Ellie could feel the warmth from him spreading out towards her. She hoped Lily was right about the tights; right now, she felt as if she might overheat. Danes kept their homes so *warm*. That was obviously the only reason her cheeks felt so hot. Nothing to do with how close Jesper was sitting.

'The hygge,' Ellie repeated, trying to focus. 'Even us Brits know about that. It's all cushions and candles and stuff, right?'

He gave her a patient smile. 'That's part of it. But more than that, it's about being cosy at home, with your family or loved ones. Like tonight. Later, we might venture out into the city to celebrate the New Year, I think. But right now, we are here, enjoying each other's company, some good food and drink, the candlelight and the companionship.' His mouth twisted a little, until his smile looked somehow sad. 'This is what I missed when I was away.'

'I suppose life in the States must have been a very different pace,' Ellie said. The Danes valued their work-life balance very highly—and she knew from experience that wasn't always the case in America.

'Uh, yes. Very different.' Jesper sounded surprised, as if he hadn't been thinking about America at all, which was curious.

He gave her another tight smile, then turned his attention to the platters of food Lily had prepared for them. Ellie followed suit, but she couldn't help wondering what he *had* been thinking about when he talked about being away.

Jesper was an interesting man. And she knew her sister, if she were there, would point out that he was an incredibly good-looking one, too.

Two things Ellie knew she'd do better to avoid, given what had happened last time she'd allowed herself to be beguiled by an interesting and gorgeous man.

But still, she had to admit she was intrigued. Intrigued and incredibly attracted.

Across the room, Lily gave her a knowing look and a small waggle of the eyebrows, and Ellie looked away—fast. The last thing she needed was her best friend getting ideas about her thinking this set-up was a good idea.

Especially since only Lily understood the real reason she was in Denmark in the dead of winter to begin with.

CHAPTER TWO

JESPER LEANED BACK into the soft welcome of Anders and Lily's sofa, side plate in hand, and watched the woman beside him with covert glances when she wasn't looking.

He had to admit, he was intrigued. Intrigued and attracted. And while the attraction was unexpected, it wasn't so surprising—Ellie was gorgeous, with her warm hazel eyes and wide smile. Something about her sparked a physical reaction in him he hadn't anticipated feeling that evening, or any time soon. But it wasn't even the most interesting thing about her.

There was something deeper inside her, something soul-deep about her that he wanted to know, to understand. And that surprised him more than anything.

It had been a very long while since a woman had intrigued him.

He wondered if that was why Anders had invited him along, knowing she'd be there. His best friend had always had an unerring sense of what would pique Jesper's curiosity, what would draw him out of his shell. It was how he'd lured him away from his studies at university, and later persuaded him to leave work for the occasional fishing trip when he'd visited them in the States, or even convinced him to come back to Denmark for high days and holidays like today.

It had been Anders who had introduced him to Agnes in the first place, of course.

Or perhaps it had been Lily. And perhaps this set-up—it hadn't escaped his notice that the other promised guests were entirely absent—was more to do with Ellie than him. Something else to wonder about.

Beside him, Ellie had turned slightly to chat with Lily, sitting on the armchair beside her, her face lit up by the candlelight. Anders' wife was a beautiful woman, made more beautiful by the way she responded to his friend's love and care. Jesper had been honestly delighted when he heard they'd married—even if he suspected that their sudden elopement and tiny wedding had been at least partially because the obvious best man hadn't been available.

In fact, Jesper had been so completely off-the-grid he hadn't heard about their wedding until three months after the fact.

Had Ellie been there? Yes, she must have been. He could see her beaming in a photo with Lily in a wedding dress, set out on one of the shelves beside the fire.

If he'd been at the wedding, they would have met there. Maybe shared a drink, flirted a little. If he still even remembered how to do that. In another world, one where he hadn't been grieving his wife, hadn't been married at all, perhaps, anything might have happened. Who knew where a little flirting might lead...

He could try tonight, he realised. Will had been right. He needed to get used to being around people again. He couldn't live the rest of his hopefully long life alone in the backwoods, like some story of a man made up to frighten school kids.

Well, he *could*. And if he was totally honest with himself—something he'd been working hard on being for the last few years—a lot of days he wanted to. But the world would still be out there, and sometimes he had to interact with it.

Maybe it was time to dip his toe back in the water of social interaction. He was certain that was what Anders and Lily had decided, which was why they'd invited him tonight at all. Unless…yes, more and more, he was convinced that this cosy double date wasn't solely for his benefit.

He gazed again at Ellie's profile in the candlelight. Lily would have told her that winter was the wrong time for her project, if she wanted to meet other Danes out in the wild. Or she'd have been able to introduce her to more people even in the coldest, darkest season, if that was the real reason Ellie was here, and there had been no other time she could visit. No, he suspected there was another reason for Ellie's sudden Danish odyssey.

Maybe she was hiding, just like he had been.

But what from?

Jesper looked away. He was not in the business of getting involved in other people's lives and problems—he never had been, but certainly not since his own life had imploded. He knew only too well that there was little you could do for others when their world fell apart. Many friends and family had reached out to help him, even those whose friendships he'd sorely neglected over the years he was consumed with building his business. But in the end, there was nothing they could do for the grief and the regrets.

All he'd been able to combat them with was time and solitude.

Well, that and a complete upheaval of everything in his life that had gone before.

He suspected that wasn't what Ellie needed. Few people ever wanted or needed the extremes he seemed to be programmed to go for. It certainly wasn't the Danish way. He was an outlier.

Or he had been. These days, he worked hard to walk that middle line. To find that balance so craved by his countrymen.

He'd learned a lot, out in the wilderness the last few years, with nothing to keep him company but his own thoughts and regrets. But, in the end, what it had taught him most was that either extreme—workaholism or dropping out and checking out—wasn't going to make him happy.

For that, he'd come back to the Danish lifestyle he'd always eschewed before as too easy, not ambitious enough.

He found it faintly ironic that it turned out his mother had been right all along. He wished she was still alive, so he could tell her so.

Maybe that was the same lesson Ellie needed to learn—not that he expected to be the person to teach her. Happiness was a personal thing.

Every person needed to find out for themselves what made them happy. Yes, there were some broad tenets that could be applied, but Jesper had never been a believer in one size fits all.

'Well, if you want to meet more Danes, there'll probably be some at the Tivoli Gardens tonight,' Anders told Ellie, excitement clear in his voice. 'I mean, many of them will still be tourists, but maybe from Denmark? Who knows? You could perform some informal interviews, perhaps?'

Ellie curled her legs under her on the sofa. It made her look curiously young—even though if she was of an age with Lily, Jesper knew she couldn't be many years younger than his own forty-eight. 'What do Danes usually do for New Year?' she asked.

'It depends,' Jesper said. 'My brother-in-law Will and his husband Matthew always throw a lavish party for their many, many friends—ending with watching the fireworks from the roof garden at midnight.'

Ellie gave him a curious look. 'And you didn't want to be there tonight?'

Jesper winced. 'Will is more my…ex-brother-in-law. Or something. I'm not really sure. Although he did invite me when I saw him earlier today. But, uh, no. I chose to be here instead.'

He wasn't sure any of that made sense, but he didn't really want to get into the issue of his widower status right now. He assumed Lily and Anders hadn't mentioned it, or Ellie wouldn't have asked the question. Indeed, Lily was giving him an awkwardly apologetic smile even now. She was British, of course. She felt a social faux pas acutely. Jesper suspected it was bred into the Brits, even now.

Her husband, meanwhile, had no sense of embarrassment or shame—something Jesper suspected he'd only become quite so sensitive to since his years in the States. He clapped Jesper on the back with a broad, firm hand. 'And that was the right decision! Or else you wouldn't have had the company of the lovely Ellie for our visit to the Tivoli Gardens winter wonderland, would you?'

'This is true.' Jesper turned to offer Ellie a friendly smile and found her already watching him, her hazel eyes wide under her fringe. She had brown hair, something Jesper would have thought fairly nondescript until now, watching all the colours hidden in it—from red to gold to umber, with silver threads coming through— shining in the candlelight.

She dipped her gaze and tucked her hair behind her ear, and Jesper took a moment to catch his breath.

Yes, there was definitely more to Ellie than he'd imagined when he'd arrived. And suddenly he knew he wouldn't sleep unless he found out what it was, and why he felt so captivated by her hazel eyes.

The Tivoli Gardens were a highlight of Copenhagen life. Lily told her that in the summer they were swarming with tourists from the moment they opened in spring to when they closed in the autumn, everyone eager to experience the rides and shows, music and spectacle. They'd been closed for the winter when Ellie had been planning her last-minute trip, but opened for a winter spectacular all over the Christmas period. This, however, was her first visit to the Copenhagen landmark.

And she had to admit it was pretty magical.

The whole place had been lit up with thousands upon thousands of tiny lights, every tree, every building, every structure, railing against the dark of a winter night. Music played—she wasn't sure from where, except that maybe it was everywhere—and children, up way past their usual bedtime, she assumed, raced around enjoying the sights and begging to go on the different rides.

Anders and Lily walked hand in hand in front of her, Lily resting her head against her new husband's upper arm as they soaked in the magic.

Ellie hung back and stuck close to Jesper, who seemed to be doing the same thing, just in case she got lost.

'It's quite something, isn't it?' Jesper said. Somehow, his voice carried through all the noise and hustle—or maybe she was just standing closer to him than she'd realised. Yes, now she checked, she was practically pressed up against his side, in her attempt not to get lost in the crowd.

She took a step to the side. 'It really is. What do you think? Does it rival the Rockefeller Center for Christmas merriment?'

Jesper rumbled a low laugh. 'I think it probably does. Although I have to admit, I never went ice-skating or whatever it is you're supposed to do there when I was in New York.'

Ellie gasped in mock horror. 'You didn't? Well, what *were* you doing there?'

'Wasting my time, clearly,' he joked back. But then, as he looked at her, his expression turned more serious, pensive even. 'Mostly I was working. All of the time.'

'Not very Danish of you.' The words popped out before Ellie could stop them, and she winced. 'Sorry. It's all this Danish happiness research I've been doing.'

'It's okay. You're right.' He gave a small shake of the head. 'I…wasn't very Danish for a long time. Not all Danes are, you realise. I mean, as a country we have a certain reputation, and most of us live up to it, but…we're all individuals as well. We need to find out for ourselves what makes us happy.'

'I *do* realise that,' Ellie replied. 'I think that's part of what makes understanding the Scandinavian happiness phenomenon so hard. I mean, I know so much has already been written about it, for years now. But I was hoping that, now the initial hype of hygge and Swedish death cleaning and everything has passed, I could find something new to say. Something real.'

'But you haven't?'

'Not yet.' Ellie sighed. 'But I still have two months. And, I mean, everyone here looks pretty happy, so there are worse places to be on New Year's Eve.'

'You're still working now, then,' Jesper

pointed out. 'On New Year's Eve. Not very Danish of *you.*'

'Ah, but I'm a writer,' Ellie countered. 'We're never not working. Inspiration doesn't work to a schedule.'

'And your inspiration—your muse, perhaps?—have they been good to you in Copenhagen?' he asked.

It was only a polite question, she knew that. Just a half-interested enquiry from a new ac- quaintance. People were always interested in her writing process, in her experience—either baffled by the very idea of wanting to get words down on paper in the first place, or because they believed they had a book in them that they'd write one day, if only they found the time.

That was what *she'd* believed. After years of writing articles and essays and posts online, she'd thought it was finally time to pull it all to- gether in a book. But here she was in Denmark, with all the time in the world and nothing to do but write, and still the words wouldn't come.

'Perhaps not as good as I had been hoping,' she offered with a small smile.

A group of young twenty-somethings ap- proaching from the opposite direction almost barrelled into them with shouted apologies after the fact, and Jesper pulled her out of their way, tucking her against his body with her arm slotted through the bend in his. She should object, she thought, to such a casual ownership of her space, her arm. But at the same time…he had protected her. Somehow, his arm around her felt…right. And the slow, low buzz of attraction that filled her at his touch was certainly keeping her warm.

'So now you're back from the States do you find you work less, here in Denmark?' Time to turn the conversation back onto him, she'd decided. Her own woeful writing work was *not* what she wanted to be focusing on this New Year's Eve.

'Far less.' Jesper huffed a small laugh, sending a cloud of steam into the night air. 'If I'm honest, I've hardly thought about business since I returned.'

Ellie frowned. She'd been expecting a line about settling back into the balanced way of working and living the Danes seemed to have sussed, but this sounded like something else. More like he'd gone from one extreme to another.

'I don't understand,' she said slowly. 'I'm sure Anders said that you had a business meeting before you came to the flat.'

'That is true.' He didn't elaborate.

Maybe she was asking the wrong questions. Or he was deliberately offering unhelpful answers.

Perhaps both.

'Why *did* you return to Denmark?'

That was clearly the right question, but she was almost sorry she'd asked it. Jesper's arm tightened around hers, and for a moment a flash of something an awful lot like pain filled his features.

'My wife died,' he said softly. 'In a car accident. I was... I was at work, of course, so she had taken a cab back from our penthouse apartment to the airport for a visit home to her family here in Denmark. And there was an accident and she died. And suddenly I didn't want to work any longer.'

Ellie squeezed his arm in reply, sudden guilt filling her for thinking that the attraction she felt in his presence might have been reciprocated. Maybe she'd been wrong about this being a set-up at all. 'I'm so sorry. I shouldn't have asked. It's the journalist in me—I'm always asking questions that people would rather I didn't.'

He shrugged. 'No, it's fine. I've got to get used to saying it. People will ask.'

'Was it very recent?' It certainly sounded that

way—raw, and as if he hadn't grown accustomed yet to sharing the awful news with others.

To a lesser extent, Ellie knew how that felt. For months after she and Dave first split up, she'd find herself forgetting that they weren't still together, especially when making plans with friends. Telling everyone had been by far the hardest part, and it seemed to go on for ever, as if there was always someone for whom it was news. And of course that just made it ache all over again.

'Agnes died three years ago now,' Jesper replied.

So, not very recent, but obviously not anywhere close to enough time to have got over the tragedy at all. He must miss her enormously, still. Perhaps they'd been together a long time—since school, or whatever. To be heading into the second half of his life without the person he'd expected to spend it with must be very hard to come to terms with.

Actually, she knew it was. Because while Dave was still very much alive, her future—the one she'd expected to live—had vanished.

'You must have loved her very much,' she said finally. 'I'm so sorry for your loss.'

God, what a New Year's Eve this was turning out to be. Two middle-aged people who couldn't seem to get over the lives they'd lost. This probably wasn't what Lily had planned for them when she'd brought them together for the evening.

Maybe it was time to call it, and head back to Britain, book or no book.

Except she couldn't. Not until after January was over, anyway.

There was no way in hell she was going to be in London until after then. Whatever her mother or half-sister said.

If she was, she knew she'd only end up going along with what they wanted her to do once again, like always. And this time, this one time... Ellie knew she couldn't do it. However unhappy it made people.

After a lifetime of people pleasing, she knew that this time she needed to stay far away. And being in Denmark gave her the perfect excuse to *not* do what her family wanted, without having to tell them how much she hated that they were asking it of her in the first place, and ruining their relationship for ever.

She couldn't leave yet.

Jesper had visited the Tivoli Gardens many times in his life, although never before at New

Year. He'd seen the fireworks though, from his brother-in-law's roof garden.

Before, he'd always resented the time taken away from more important things. Tonight, however, he felt certain that there was nothing more important that he could be doing than talking to Ellie.

She fascinated him—far more now they'd started talking than when he was merely watching her back at the apartment. It wasn't just the hum of instant attraction that he felt between them. This was something more.

The way she asked questions. The line that formed between her eyebrows when she tried to figure out his answers and what they meant. He knew, instinctively, that this was a woman who had lived a full life to this point—she was brimming with it. And yet, all that enthusiasm and life seemed to be tucked neatly away inside her winter coat, as if she were afraid to let it out again.

No wonder she was having trouble finding enough happiness to write about. The woman was clearly *un*happy, even if she didn't seem willing to admit it—to him, or to her friends. She plastered on a smile over the cracks of her misery, and everyone seemed willing to accept that as reality.

Everyone except him.

Why?

Maybe they genuinely didn't see it. Or perhaps they already knew what she was covering and understood that was what she needed to do right now. He didn't feel he could ask Lily: announcing that her friend was miserable and how could she not have noticed, wasn't exactly the best vibe for a New Year's Eve celebration.

And yet...he couldn't help thinking about it. Why would a woman so patently unhappy be writing a book about happiness?

They paused beside the ice rink, watching the skaters glide in circles around the ice, under the sparkling lights and the branches of the nearby trees. Lily and Anders had disappeared to explore the many food stalls, promising to bring back delights to supplement the nibbles they'd had back at the apartment. Jesper had been tempted by the aromas drifting from some of the nearest wooden stalls, but in the end elected to stay with Ellie and watch the skating.

She rested her forearms on the white metal railing that surrounded the rink and Jesper followed suit, carefully avoiding the garland spotted with fairy lights that hung from it.

'They look happy, don't they?' Ellie observed, staring out at the skaters.

'Going round and round in circles and getting nowhere? I suppose they do.' Jesper had meant it as a joke, something to lighten the mood, but the more he thought about it, the more true it felt.

'That was me, before, I suppose,' she said thoughtfully, almost as if she hadn't meant to speak out loud at all. When he looked at her, waiting for more, she gave a small, embarrassed smile and looked back out over the rink again. 'I mean, I think it's very easy to live your life and think you have everything sorted, but then something happens that means you look at it all differently...'

'And realise that you were just treading water,' Jesper finished, when she trailed off. 'Or skating in circles.'

'Exactly.' She gripped the edge of the railing tight, then leaned back, her feet anchoring her on the step at the bottom of the railing, her body stretching out to form a triangle. She reminded him of a child, swinging off the bars in a playground, perhaps. For the first time since he'd met her earlier that evening, she seemed... free.

But then the moment was over and Ellie stood straight against the railing again, a wistful look in her eye.

'Would you like to try?' Jesper suggested, motioning out towards the skaters.

For a moment, he thought she might be considering it. But then she bit her lip and shook her head. 'We should go and find Lily and Anders. Besides, I'd probably just fall over. It's years since I've been ice-skating.'

'All the more reason to do it, then,' he said. 'Not the falling part, obviously. I'll go with you, if you want.'

She glanced up at him in surprise, and for a moment he could see worlds in her eyes. A life lived where just wanting to do something wasn't enough reason to do it, and where no one ever offered to just go along for the ride.

He got the impression that Ellie had spent far more of her life so far doing what others wanted or expected her to do than chasing after her own wishes and dreams.

'Sometimes skating in circles can be fun,' he said softly. 'We don't always have to be trying to get somewhere.'

'I suppose.' She held his gaze for a long moment, those expressive hazel eyes telling whole novels he could only read snippets of. Then she looked away and smiled—not the real one he'd been hoping to surprise from her though, but another of those fake plastered-over smiles—

and he knew the moment was over. 'Lily, Anders!' She waved their friends over as they approached with trays of food, then she hopped down from the step by the ice rink to approach them.

Jesper followed more slowly behind. Ellie had wanted to go skating, but she'd stopped herself. He wondered who had told her she couldn't do the things she wanted to do. Wondered how she ever expected to be happy if she didn't.

Wondered if maybe, maybe, he could be the person to change that belief.

The night darkened and deepened as midnight approached, it seemed, even though the sun had been down for hours. Full of street food from the stalls—including some delicious desserts Jesper hadn't been able to resist, and had been totally worth it for the sight of Ellie licking chocolate sauce from the corner of her mouth—they wandered the busy paths of the gardens to find the best spot to watch the fireworks from. Obviously, they weren't the only people trying to do that so competition was fierce.

'They'll be up in the sky, you realise,' Anders pointed out as Lily rejected yet another site as not quite right. 'We'll be able to see them wherever we are.'

'I know. It's just—ooh! Let's try over there!' And Lily was off again, chasing another spot that might be perfect, tugging Ellie along behind her.

Jesper shared a fondly exasperated look with his friend as they followed.

Finally, Lily was satisfied, and the four of them settled in with moments to spare to watch the iconic firework display, which fired at eleven so as not to conflict with the other firework displays around town at midnight. This suited Jesper perfectly; it meant they could be back in the safety of Anders and Lily's flat before the midnight madness started and *everyone* in Copenhagen seemed to want to set off fireworks.

Of course, they weren't the only ones to find this area around the open-air stage the perfect place to view from, so they found themselves surrounded by others, oohing and ahhing as the first fireworks split the skies.

Ellie was jostled towards him again and Jesper put an arm around her, holding her against his side. He glanced down to check that she was okay and she gave him a shy smile, before jumping as another loud firework exploded.

Her attention was drawn quickly back to the sky, and Jesper knew he should be watching the fireworks, too. But somehow, he found himself watching *her* watching them instead. Seeing the wonder and joy in her eyes as golds and reds and greens and whites cascaded across the night sky.

This, he felt certain, was a woman capable of great happiness.

And part of him really wanted to be the one to show her how to find it.

Just for a little while.

CHAPTER THREE

THE FIREWORKS WERE, Ellie had to admit, spectacular. Still, part of her was secretly glad when they were over and it was time to head back to Anders and Lily's flat to ring in the New Year with champagne and toasts. She tried to convince herself that it was just because she was cold and the crowds were growing a little oppressive, but she knew the truth was that she wasn't sure how much longer she could spend pressed up against Jesper's side without starting to get ideas.

Find a hot guy to kiss at midnight for me! Sarah had said in her message. And suddenly, Ellie was beginning to think that her sister had the right idea.

Which was a clear sign that she should probably say no to another glass of champagne when they got home.

'Are you okay?' Lily asked, as they made their way out of the park and back to the flat.

She had her arm through Ellie's like they'd used to do at university, walking home from pubs and clubs late at night, sharing secrets and gossip from their night out. It made Ellie feel twenty again, instead of more than double that. Where *had* the years gone? 'Ellie?' Lily asked again, and she realised she hadn't answered her friend's question.

'I'm fine,' she promised. 'Just thinking. About the new year ahead, you know.' That sounded better than admitting she was growing maudlin about all the years gone by, lost to them for ever.

'And who you might *kiss* at New Year?' Lily whispered, giggling very close to Ellie's ear.

Ellie glared at her. 'Has Sarah been texting you too?'

'Maybe.' Lily tried to keep a poker face and failed. Miserably. 'But mostly I was just thinking how nice it was to see you and Jesper talking tonight…'

'He's a good conversationalist.' She resolutely did not elaborate on the way his bright blue eyes seemed to see past all of her defences, or how incredibly good his arm felt around her when they walked together. 'I'm glad I wasn't the third wheel for you and Anders tonight. You know, since everyone else *cancelled* on you.'

Lily beamed, looking utterly unrepentant

about her set-up plans. 'Oh, good! I know you don't like it when we spring people on you, and I know things are…sensitive at the moment. But I had a feeling the two of you would get on. And besides, if you're looking for a Dane to talk about happiness… Jesper has been on both sides of that equation. He could be really good for your book, if you're still looking for more material.'

'Maybe,' Ellie allowed. She wasn't about to admit how little material she had—to Lily *or* to Jesper, for that matter. It was just too humiliating.

Back at the flat, Anders cracked open the champagne and they all stood at the tiny barred balcony outside the living room window and counted down to midnight, their glasses held ready.

'Ten!' Lily had jumped up onto the sofa to get a better view over their heads, and was in danger of spilling her champagne.

'Nine!' Anders wrapped an arm around her waist and steadied her.

'Eight!' Ellie looked up and shared a smile with Jesper at their friends' antics.

'Seven!' Her breath caught as her gaze met his.

'Six!' She was still counting. How was she

still counting when all she could think about was his eyes?

'Five!' It must be muscle memory, her lips still moving as they knew they should, even as her brain started to short-circuit.

'Four!' This was all Sarah's fault. And Lily's. She'd never have even thought of kissing a virtual stranger at midnight if they hadn't suggested it.

'Three!' And now it was all that she could think about.

'Two!' She licked her lips between numbers, and saw Jesper's throat bob as he swallowed. He didn't look away though.

'One!' Maybe she wasn't the only one thinking about midnight kisses. Maybe...

'Happy New Year!' They all yelled it together as, outside, more fireworks boomed and crackled and exploded. Ellie didn't need to look back to see that Anders and Lily were wrapped around each other in a joyous embrace.

She couldn't look, anyway. She could only see Jesper's bright blue eyes.

'Happy New Year, Ellie,' he whispered, and she tried to smile, tried to respond in kind, but couldn't.

He leaned in, obviously aiming for her cheek to kiss, but then hesitated as he grew closer.

One hand came up to cup her cheek and, as his gaze met hers again, she gave what she thought was probably an imperceptible nod.

Jesper saw it, though. And his kiss didn't land on her cheek.

As his lips met hers, Ellie tried to relax, to sink into the feeling, but she couldn't shake the thought that this was her first kiss since her divorce. Her first post-Dave kiss.

There had been so many firsts since they'd separated—first birthday alone, first night in her own place, first solo dinner out—but this one, oh, this one she could enjoy.

She leaned into it now, feeling his lips curve against hers in a smile as she kissed him back. And for the first time in a long time, Ellie Peters began to feel alive.

Two days into the new year, she was still thinking about that kiss.

No, not the kiss. Well, not *just* the kiss.

She was remembering what Jesper had murmured to her as they'd parted later that night, or in the early hours really—him heading back to his hotel and Ellie setting up camp on Lily and Anders' pull-out bed for what was left of the night.

'It's been most interesting to meet you, Ellie,'

he'd said. 'And…if you ever want any help finding that path to happiness, give me a call.'

She'd raised an eyebrow at the obvious line and he'd chuckled, shaking his head.

'Not like that. I just mean…happiness and how to find it is something I've spent a lot of time thinking about and working on personally, since my wife died. I'd be happy to discuss it further, if you'd like.'

He'd nodded once more and walked away— leaving Ellie remembering the fact that she'd just kissed—quite passionately—an obviously still grieving widower, and feeling icky about the whole thing.

So she'd tried—unsuccessfully—to put it out of her mind.

But two days later, with three unanswered emails from her agent in her inbox, all asking how the book was going, Ellie was getting desperate.

Then, worse, the phone rang. Not just a message or an email, but an actual phone call. Ellie had almost forgotten that people even did that.

She checked the caller ID before answering, obviously, but she was certain it would be her agent—until she saw the name scrolling across her screen and groaned.

This was worse. Far worse.

The ringing stopped, then started up again mere moments later.

Ellie took a deep breath and answered.

'Hi, Mum. Sorry—it rang off just before I could get to it.'

'Hmm.' Her mother didn't sound convinced. 'Well, I've got you now—and it's just as well. There are a million things we need to talk about before the wedding!'

The wedding. The whole reason she'd run away to another country to begin with.

'Mum, I can't make the wedding. I told you that. I'm in Denmark for work, remember?' A trip that had been arranged almost entirely around the premise of being out of the country for the January wedding date, and the run-up to it.

'Oh, Ellie.' Her mother had that half pitying, half 'I know you better than yourself' tone that Ellie hated, and she knew that this was not going to be a good phone call. 'I know you said you wouldn't be able to get back for it, but Tom and I are happy to help with the airfare if that's the problem.'

'That's not the problem, Mum.' And, quite frankly, if her mother couldn't see what the real problem was… Ellie had very little hope for the human race.

No, her mum knew full well why Ellie didn't want to be there. She was just trying to ignore it.

She was so used to barrelling through and expecting Ellie to toe the family line to keep the peace, to keep everyone happy, that she couldn't see that this demand was an ask too far. That what she wanted this time was so far over the line that nobody in their right mind would ask her to do it.

Well, unless they'd spent forty-four years with Ellie doing exactly what they asked, every time, because it was easier than having a fight, or dealing with her mum getting upset or throwing a tantrum.

Ellie *knew* she'd brought this situation on herself. But it didn't make it any easier to deal with.

'Ellie, I think you're being very oversensitive about this,' her mum said. 'We all do!'

Ellie wondered who 'all' were. She could guess though. Her older sister Sarah, for instance, didn't think she was being oversensitive. She'd come over to help her pack and made cocktails while they did it.

No, 'all' would be her mum, her stepfather Tom and her half-sister Maisie who, at twenty-two, was proving to be quite the Bridezilla.

And Ellie knew exactly *why* they all wanted her there too. To stop the gossip. To prove they were one big, happy family and everything was fine. But they weren't, and everything wasn't.

'I'm not being oversensitive,' Ellie said, as calmly as she could manage. 'But I'm also not coming home for the wedding. I'm doing important work over here, and I'm going to keep doing it.'

Her mother scoffed. 'Important work? Writing about *happiness*, when you're ruining the happiest day of your sister's life?'

'Half-sister,' Ellie replied. Normally, she'd have left it there. But she was feeling...different since New Year. As if maybe she could take a stand in her own life, for once. So she didn't keep her next words confined to her own internal monologue. 'And, in fairness, she ruined my marriage first.'

For one blissful moment her mother was shocked into silence. Sadly, it didn't last. 'Ellie, you know that's not true. Maisie and Dave only got together after you two had split up. Everything was totally above board. But you not showing up at the wedding gives the wrong message about that. Maisie's very upset at the idea that people might think you don't give them your blessing.'

I don't, Ellie's mind screamed. *I don't give*

*them my blessing. My ex-husband is marry-
ing my half-sister—who is also half my age—
and I am not okay with that. I don't see why I
should be.*

But she couldn't say any of that to her mum.
Not even now, not even when she knew she
should.

Keeping the peace in her family was far too
ingrained in her to go that far.

'I'm not getting any younger you know, love,'
her mum said, despite the fact that, at sixty-
seven, Tracey Peters had more energy than
Ellie had possessed in years. 'I just want to
see all my girls together and happy. Is that so
wrong?'

Ellie sighed. There was no way she was
going to win this argument, anyway. She never
had. Why start a fight now when she knew
she'd never win? 'No, Mum.'

'So you'll come?'

No. Not in a million years.

'I'll…see what I can do.' Ellie hated herself
for even saying it, but she knew she'd never get
off the phone otherwise.

'That's all I ask.' Her mum managed to
sound suitably martyred, even though Ellie
knew full well that was *not* all she asked, and

anything less than doing things exactly her way would never be tolerated.

She'd hoped that putting significant air miles between them would help her escape the guilt trips. Apparently, she'd been wrong.

But maybe it would at least help Ellie to avoid caving in.

Mum mollified, she managed to get off the phone after only another fifteen minutes of unwanted updates on what every single one of Tracey's acquaintances was up to. As she pressed the end call button, Ellie lowered her head to her arms on her desk and focused on just breathing in the quiet for a moment or two.

Then her email pinged with another message from her agent.

This was ridiculous. She had to do *something*. About the book, about the wedding, about her *life*.

And right now, she could only think of one thing she *could* do.

So she picked up her phone and messaged Lily to ask for Jesper's phone number.

Jesper hadn't been expecting to hear from Ellie again. Hoping, sure. But not expecting.

These days, he tried not to expect too much from other people. He knew that the only person who could shape his reality was himself, and so he relied only on himself, as far as possible.

And Will, he supposed, when it came to financial matters.

And Anders, and by extension Lily, to keep him anchored to the wider world.

And now maybe, maybe, Ellie, just a little bit. To feel useful. As if what he'd learned in the last few years could be of service to more people than just himself.

It had been a strange impulse that led him to invite her to get in touch to discuss happiness, if she wanted, for her book. He'd been a little shaken by the kiss, if he was honest with himself—and he did try to be, these days. He hadn't kissed a woman since Agnes' death, and he hadn't expected to that night, for all of Will's teasing and the strange draw he felt towards Ellie. At most, he'd have imagined a peck on the cheek—or maybe lips, if he was feeling daring.

But instead…instead he'd found himself drawn in by her, until the planned brush of his lips against hers turned into something far deeper. A lingering kiss that had stirred something inside him he'd thought lost. A kiss that he just had to deepen, that called for him to wrap his arms tighter around Ellie's waist and hold her against him.

A kiss he knew he wouldn't forget in a hurry.

So maybe that was why he'd told her to call, if she wanted. He didn't have her number, and wouldn't ask Lily or Anders for it without Ellie's permission, so the ball was in her court. She could find him, through their mutual friends, if she wanted to—and she had the excuse of it being for work. It was all up to her.

He hadn't really expected to hear from her again, though. Certainly not a mere two days later.

Jesper had to admit, seeing her text message had lifted his spirits rather, though.

Fortunately, he was still in Copenhagen when she messaged, having spent the holiday catching up on some reading and walking around the quiet city, before a more in-depth meeting with Will on the first working day of the year.

And now, the day after Ellie's message, he was sitting in one of his favourite Copenhagen cafés, waiting for her to join him for pastries and coffee.

He was early—he usually was—so he had the luxury of watching for her, and seeing her pause outside the café window, checking her phone, presumably to confirm that she was in the right place. Then, with a small nod to herself, she pushed the door open and stepped inside, scanning the tables for him.

She looked much as she had on New Year's Eve, as they'd toured the Tivoli Gardens, her sunny yellow bobble hat pulled down over her still mostly dark hair. He'd seen strands of silver glinting in the fairy lights when she'd taken it off that night, although not nearly so many as peppered his temples and beard. He liked them. They gave her a faintly ethereal air, somehow.

Or maybe he just liked that she wasn't trying to stay—or at least look—forever young. Agnes had spent a fortune—in time, money and energy—keeping time at bay, but in the end, all of that time she'd keep fending off came for her at once. Nowadays, Jesper appreciated the signs of ageing, of still being in the world, all the more.

Jesper half stood, waved, and smiled when she caught sight of him and her shoulders visibly relaxed as she hurried over to his table. They did the awkward greeting of two people who had only met once—but had already kissed—before she took the seat opposite him.

'Hi,' she said again, looking faintly embarrassed for reasons he didn't fully understand. 'Thanks for doing this.'

'Of course. Let me go get you some coffee and pastries, and we can start.' Even if he wasn't entirely sure what they were starting.

Ellie started to get up, reaching for her purse. 'I can get them! I mean, you're here helping me...'

Jesper waved her away. 'Think of it as a welcome to Copenhagen.' Even if she'd been there two months already, she looked so ill at ease, he thought she still counted as a newcomer.

It didn't take long to procure a plate piled high with various specialities and return to the table. Ellie's eyes widened at the sight of all the pastries and sweet treats.

'I wasn't sure what you'd already tried and what you haven't,' he explained. 'So I got one of everything. Plus, this bakery is my *favourite*, and I'll be leaving Copenhagen to head home again tomorrow, so I need to get my fill while I'm here.'

'You don't live in Copenhagen?' Ellie reached tentatively for a *kanelsnegle*—a cinnamon swirl—and he gave her an encouraging nod.

'Not any more, no. I grew up here, though I lived in other parts of the country at different times. Then I moved to the States after my

marriage, and back to Denmark again after—'
He broke off. They were here to talk about
happiness. He didn't want to frighten her off
too soon by mentioning his wife's death again.
Even if it *had* been the thing that set him back
on the right path.

Ellie didn't miss a beat. 'But not to Copenhagen. So where?'

'I have a house out on the coast, up in North
Jutland. About four hours' drive away from
here.' And a world away from everywhere, it
always seemed, when he was there. Which was
why he loved it so much, of course.

She nodded, obviously computing as she
chewed. 'That's about how long it used to take
us to get to visit my grandparents from London as a kid. It seemed like for ever then, but
now... I suppose it's not so far. These pastries
are amazing, by the way.'

'Try the jam *spandauer*,' he suggested, point-
ing to the jam-filled pastry with icing sugar
sprinkled over it. 'They were always my favourite when I was small.'

'If you insist.' She didn't sound as if he was
twisting her arm. 'So, now you only come to
Copenhagen for business? Or to visit friends?'

'Yes, I suppose. I hadn't been back much
before this trip, I must confess.' He smiled at

the sight of her face as she took her first bite, icing sugar powdering her top lip. 'I'm glad I did, though.'

'So am I.' Ellie licked away the sugar, and Jesper felt a new warmth rise up in him as his mind filled with memories of their kiss.

It was possible he was in more trouble here than he'd anticipated.

For a moment, Ellie forgot how incredible the Danish pastries tasted and lost herself in Jesper's bright blue eyes once more, just as she had on New Year's Eve.

Oh, this was a bad idea. She'd known it when she'd asked Lily for his number, been certain when he'd responded to her text with the suggestion that they meet here at the café, and had almost turned back twice on her way there.

She needed to get this situation back on track. She needed his professional help, that was all. This was business, not pleasure.

Well, except for the pastries. *They* were pure pleasure.

Ellie looked away, swallowed the last mouthful of her jam-filled pastry—good, but not as incredible as the cinnamon swirl—and gathered her thoughts. She was here to ask him about happiness.

'So, moving back to Denmark, the house up in Jutland…they were part of your…um… happiness quest, after your loss?' She'd done a little research before their meeting—she was a reporter after all, and if he was going to be her source, she needed to know he was the real deal.

She'd started with a quick internet search, which had told her all about his high-flying business career in the States, and the tragic death of his wife three years earlier. Ellie had jotted down all the facts and figures—and then she'd called Lily again for the real story. Like where Jesper had been for the three years since then, and why he suddenly believed he was some sort of guru of happiness.

Lily had been reluctant to say much, insisting that if Jesper wanted to work with her on her project then it would be better for him to share the story with Ellie directly. But she had managed to get some fundamentals out of her friend.

Like the fact that, after his wife's death, Jesper had gone basically off-grid for years on some sort of personal happiness quest. Not massively unlike the one Ellie herself was *supposed* to be undertaking for her book, except that Jesper seemed to have actually done it properly.

'After Agnes died, I needed to get away from everything for a while.' Jesper spoke slowly, his broad fingers systematically shredding a cinnamon swirl onto the plate in front of him. It was a chronic waste of a pastry, but Ellie didn't interrupt him. This was what she'd come here to hear. 'I needed to…reset, perhaps. To reevaluate…everything.'

Ellie took a sip of her coffee before murmuring, 'I can understand that.'

Hadn't she needed to do the same? Wasn't that what she was *supposed* to be doing here in Copenhagen?

She just hadn't been very good at it so far.

Jesper's gaze turned sharp as he looked at her. 'Why did you really come to Denmark, Ellie?'

She blinked. 'I told you. The book. And this was the only time that fit with my schedule. Why? Did…did Lily say something?'

Lily, of course, knew all about the wedding. But if she suspected the timing of her trip had more to do with her ex marrying again, she hadn't mentioned it. And Ellie didn't want to talk about it either—especially not to Jesper, who seemed to genuinely enjoy her company.

If he knew what a pathetic, people-pleasing runaway she was, that might change.

Better that, though, than admitting how her husband had cast her aside for her half-sister, who was bright and perky and twenty-two—all the things Ellie could never be again.

'Lily didn't say anything,' Jesper assured her. 'It just seemed to me… You came all this way, to Denmark, for four whole months. But you don't really seem to be doing anything different here than you would at home in London. Am I wrong?'

Ellie swallowed, and looked away. 'Not… wrong. I just…' She broke off with a sigh.

After a long pause, Jesper said, 'You don't have to tell me your reasons, Ellie. But I will listen if you want to. Perhaps…perhaps we might be able to help each other.'

'What do *you* need help with?' she blurted out. 'I thought you had this happiness thing all sorted. That you were some kind of guru or something.'

He laughed at that. 'Not a guru. But I have managed to find some…contentment in my life, of a sort I don't think I had before. Happiness, maybe. The problem *I* have is bringing that new mindset back into the real world again, and holding onto it once normality resumes.'

'Lily said you went off-grid,' Ellie offered. 'Is that true?'

'Essentially.' Jesper popped a segment of his destroyed cinnamon swirl into his mouth.

'Like…no people, no news, no internet kind of off-grid?' she pressed. 'Is that what you think *I* need to do to find happiness? Because while the no people bit sounds good, I kind of need the internet for my job…'

'No, no. That was what I needed. It might not be right for you. And now I need to find my way back, so…no. I don't think you need to go completely off-grid to find happiness. Nor does anyone.'

'Well, that's a relief.' Ellie tilted her head as she studied him. 'So, what *do* you think I need to do? I mean, if it's not what you did, why do you think you can show me how to find the famous Danish happiness?'

'I don't know if I can,' Jesper admitted. 'But I can show you the places that brought me joy in my darkest moments. The ones that made me think about the world in a different light. The ones that brought me back to the self I thought I'd lost when Agnes died—before, even, when I was giving everything I had to my job and neglecting the people who made life worthwhile. People, you see, are everything.'

'Says the man who lived away from them for, what—two, three years?' Ellie shook her head. 'Not a ringing endorsement of people, is it? Besides, the one promise I made to myself when I came here was that any happiness I found wouldn't be dependent on other people. I've been burnt trying to find happiness in others before, and I'm never doing it again.'

He raised an eyebrow. 'Never? There's a story there, I assume?'

'There is. But not one I'm ready to share with you just yet.' God, who was she right now? She barely recognised herself, being so open and yet also setting her boundaries. This was everything all those motivational podcasts Lily kept recommending told her to do—and everything she'd never managed before in her life. Before, she'd worked hard at saying what other people wanted to hear, winning them over to her with give and take—although mostly giving, if she was honest with herself.

Which was why, of course, her mother still believed she might actually attend her half-sister's wedding to her own ex-husband. She'd never said no before, for fear of ruining those always fraught relationships with her loved ones.

But she and Jesper didn't *have* a relationship. They barely even knew each other, and once she left Denmark it was probable that she'd never see him again. Maybe that was why it was easier with him.

He must have felt that too, because he gave a small nod and said, 'That's fair. Maybe one day you'll want to tell me—but if you don't, I respect that, too.'

'Good answer.' The words popped out without her meaning to say them.

He smiled. 'I try to respond to people the way I wish they'd respond to me, these days. And I know all about not having the capacity to share terrible things, sometimes.'

They exchanged a small smile, and Ellie realised that, unlike most people in her life, this was someone she *could* imagine sharing her feelings about Dave's upcoming wedding with. Her suspicions that, whatever everybody said, the relationship between him and Maisie had started long before their marriage had officially ended. The experience of being cut loose in her forties and just not knowing where to go.

She could talk to him about that, perhaps. One day. But not yet.

'So,' Jesper said. 'If your happiness quest isn't about other people, what *is* it going to be about? Because, I have to admit, the Danes put a lot of focus on community and family. If you

don't want to write about that, you're going to
need something else, right?'

'Right.' Her brain whirred as she tried to
order her thoughts, all the possibilities and
ideas that were flying at her. For the first time,
she felt excited about this project again. Maybe
this wasn't *quite* the direction that she'd promised her publisher in her proposal, but she knew
it was what she needed right now—and maybe
other people, readers, would need it too.

It wasn't as if anything else was working,
anyway. So what would it hurt to try?

'I think what I need,' she said slowly, choosing her words with care, 'is to experience a little of what you did over the past few years. I
need to go…not off-grid exactly, but, well, *out
there*. I need to see what you saw. What helped
you find contentment and peace—and made
you want to reconnect with people when you
came out the other side.'

He raised both eyebrows. 'Is your book about
me now?'

'Not exactly. But maybe a bit?' She could
use his story to frame certain chapters, perhaps. And, if nothing else, the Denmark he
showed her could make for some good descrip-
tive prose. Make it more of a journey of dis-

covery than just a story of her sitting around in Copenhagen's cafés failing to talk to people.

The whole idea was crazy, she knew that. But she also knew in her bones that she had to try, or she'd regret it for ever.

Ellie *couldn't* go back to London with her tail between her legs—no book, no plans, no money. And even her mother couldn't expect her to attend the damn wedding if she was semi off the grid in the most remote parts of Denmark, could she?

She took a breath, and then took her chance. 'So, what do you say? Are you willing to show me *your* Denmark—and how you found happiness in it?'

CHAPTER FOUR

JESPER'S HEAD WAS screaming at him just how bad an idea this was.

But his gut was telling him it could be interesting. Important, even.

And these days, Jesper made a point of listening to his gut.

He took a long sip of his cooling coffee to consider his options. Oh, he was going to do it, that much was certain. But he knew himself. He needed rules—guidelines, at least—to make sure this didn't pull him under again. His even keel existence was hard won, and he knew that anything that made him list too far to one side or another would destroy him.

Happiness was a step further than what he'd found for himself. Jesper had chosen contentment, which was an altogether more manageable level of joy. Would that be enough for Ellie and her book? He didn't know.

On the other end of the spectrum, while he

knew how important other people were to long-lasting wellbeing, he hadn't managed to work up to letting himself get too close to anyone again just yet. Even with Will or Anders, he knew he was holding back, not going into too many details about how he was really coping, or every emotion that had almost pulled him under over the past few years.

If he expected, or even wanted, Ellie to share her secrets with him, he knew she'd want him to do the same in return, and he wasn't sure that was something he could offer.

The basics, those were easy.

I had a wife. I loved her. She died, tragically. I grieved, and I took time away to cope with my grief. In the process, I found a joy in life I hadn't expected.

Maybe that *would* be enough. The people reading these kinds of books and articles seldom wanted the messy details. They wanted the soundbites, the easily actionable items to bring them the same results.

He didn't have to share anything he didn't want to, just like Ellie.

Especially not the details on how he'd failed his marriage, long before it was over. Or how guilty he felt, every single day, for the way Agnes had died. She didn't need to know about the screaming fights or the nights he'd just stayed at the office rather than facing what was waiting for him at home. Or how he'd spent every year of their marriage knowing what she wanted from him but also realising how impossible it was for him to give.

He had never been enough for Agnes. Never been able to live up to her expectations.

Why on earth would he think he could live up to anyone else's?

But Ellie wasn't looking for a happy-ever-after from him. Hell, she wasn't even looking for a relationship.

She just needed someone to help her with her research. And Jesper had to admit it would be good to have a sense of purpose again, even if only for a little while.

'Okay,' he said after a pause he knew had been too long, but hopefully convinced her he was taking this seriously. 'I'll do it. But we need to do it my way.'

Ellie huffed what might have been a laugh. If it was, Jesper was certain she was laughing at herself. 'Has to be better than my way, given my current progress.'

'The book isn't going well, then?' That didn't surprise him.

She reached out for another pastry. 'Honestly? It's not going at all. I've been able to keep up my social media presence and convince everyone that I'm out here uncovering the secrets of a great life, but in reality… I've got nothing.'

'Nothing?'

'Not a single page.' She looked lighter just for saying it, as if the admission was freeing somehow. 'I haven't written a word of the book since the original proposal I wrote two years ago, before everything went to hell.'

'Hell?'

She looked up sharply, her eyes hunted. 'One of those things we're not talking about yet.'

'All right.' A picture was forming, even without her telling the story. *Something* had blown her life up recently—maybe not as comprehensively as his, but enough. Given the way her right hand was fiddling with the empty ring finger of her left, he suspected it had something to do with a husband—or, more likely, ex-husband.

'So, what are your rules?' she asked.

'Guidelines,' he replied. 'Not rules.'

'Fine, guidelines. What are they?'

Yes, that was a good question. What *were* they? He'd decided that he needed them, but trying to put them into words was another thing altogether.

Maybe he really had been out of society for too long. He'd forgotten how to communicate effectively.

'I can't promise that I'll find you happiness,' he said slowly. 'That's the first thing you have to understand. I can show you the places I went, tell you what I found there—what I discovered about myself. But happiness—contentment, really—is a personal thing.'

She nodded. 'I get that. And honestly... I'm not really expecting to find joy, or contentment, or happiness on this trip. I just need something to write about.'

That made it easier, he supposed. Less pressure. But it still made him a little sad to hear.

'What else?' she pressed.

'That's the main one, I guess. A disclaimer, really. Other than that... I'll need a few days here to get everything in order before we can go. And once we're on the road... I might need time alone sometimes. I'm not really used to socialising on a daily basis yet.'

She smirked. 'That one is definitely not a problem. I'm kind of an introvert these days, too.'

Something occurred to him. 'Last one,' he promised. 'You have to go along with the places I want to take you to, and the things I suggest you try. Otherwise, what's the point of all this?'

'That's fair.' She pulled a face as she said it, though, and he knew it would be a struggle for her not to argue with him about some of them. Already he was forming a mental list of the destinations and activities for their road trip of joy.

He found himself strangely looking forward to it. Far more than he'd expected to.

'I have one rule—sorry, guideline—too,' Ellie blurted out suddenly, and he wondered how long she'd been thinking it over while he spoke.

'Of course. What is it?'

'On New Year's Eve…we…well… What happened on New Year's Eve…' She trailed off again, and Jesper took pity on her.

'You mean the kiss we shared?'

'Yes.' There was the faintest pink flush to her cheeks that made Jesper want to kiss her again, just to see if he could get it to deepen. Had she been thinking about it as much as he had? If so, their adventures together might be even more fun than he'd hoped…

'That can't happen again,' she said, shattering his growing optimism. 'It was…just a New Year thing. A midnight kiss, right? But even if it were anything more, if we're going to do this happiness trip, we can only be friends. Because, like I told you—'

'You can't have your happiness rely on another person,' he finished, to show he'd been listening. 'I understand. Really, I do.' Which wasn't the same as *liking* it, but he had to admit she was probably right. Neither of them was in a good enough place for getting tangled up in something *more* than friends to be a good idea. 'Just friends.'

Even if another kiss might have convinced him of the value of being back in the world far more than all the fairy lights and fireworks of New Year's Eve had managed. He couldn't give any more than he'd already agreed to— so it wasn't fair to ask for any more from her.

'So, we're going to do this?' There was a hint of excitement in her voice that made him smile. 'We're going to go hunt down happiness together?'

He raised another pastry—this one filled with custard and icing—and held it up to her in a toast until she met it with her own chocolate laden one.

'We are,' he said, and smiled.

Deciding to go on some sort of Danish epic quest for joy was one thing. Actually doing it, Ellie was rapidly discovering, was something else.

For instance, what was she even supposed to pack? She didn't know exactly where they were going still, despite the map Jesper had pulled up on his phone in the café to demonstrate his proposed route.

'Just take everything,' Lily said when she called to strategize with her best friend. 'Jesper's car is a decent size. It's not like you're flying.'

In a way, it would be easier if they were. But apparently everywhere Jesper wanted to go in Denmark—which seemed to be almost everywhere—was drivable. Which, Ellie was realising now, meant a lot of hours trapped in a car together, with nothing to do but talk.

Somehow, she suspected she wasn't going to have many secrets left by the end of this trip.

That was only fair, really. She wanted him to spill his guts and give her everything she needed about his years in the wild to add to her book on happiness. It only made sense that he'd want a little openness and truth from her in return.

Even if she wasn't looking forward to sharing the humiliating part about her ex's wedding, and how she ran away to another country to avoid it.

Eventually, she took Lily's advice and shoved almost everything she'd brought from Britain for her four months stay back into her large suitcase and called it good, just in time to grab her coat and layer up to lug it down the stairs to where Jesper's car was waiting outside.

'Got everything?' he asked as he hefted the suitcase into the boot without breaking a sweat.

'This country of yours requires a lot of layers,' she replied, earning a laugh.

Ellie settled into the comfortable passenger seat, familiarising herself with the layout of the car she assumed she was going to be calling home for most of the next three weeks.

That was how long Jesper had estimated it would take them to cover all the ground he wanted to show her. It meant she'd be back in Copenhagen just before the wedding in London, but she was hoping she could fudge the timings on that when she made her next round of excuses to her mother.

'No satnav?' she asked as he pulled away from the kerb and she realised he had no guidance for where they were going.

'Don't need it,' he replied. 'I'm going home. How could I lose my way?'

Since Ellie had once managed to get lost between the tube station and the office she walked to every day, just because one tiny stretch of pavement had been closed and she'd had to take a slight detour, she wasn't sure she had his faith in a person's ability to unerringly find their way home. But as Jesper took turns and roads confidently on his way out of the city, it became clear that he, at least, could do it.

He had some music playing—something light, unobtrusive, something that would allow for as much conversation as they wanted, but Ellie found herself listening to it too deeply, perhaps to avoid talking at all.

Or perhaps because she was in a strange car with a strange man going to a strange place and, really, wasn't that a little bit extreme to avoid telling her mother she wouldn't go to her half-sister's wedding?

'Are you having second thoughts?' Jesper asked after a while. Ellie wasn't sure when he'd learned to read her mind, but she didn't like it. Or was she just that much of an open book?

'Not second thoughts,' she lied. 'Just thoughts.'

'Such as?'

'Where exactly are we going first?' She'd text Lily the details, just in case. Oh, she trusted Jesper—and so did Anders and Lily, or she wouldn't be going in the first place. But if something happened, something went wrong, someone should know where she was.

And she definitely wasn't telling her mother. She wouldn't put it past Tracey Peters to be on the first flight out there to haul her home again if she thought she was running away again.

'I'm going to take you to my home, in Jutland,' Jesper said. 'It's where I went first when…when I returned to this country.'

When his wife died, Ellie's mind filled in for her.

Was it strange that she was relying on someone in such a different situation to help her find happiness? Jesper had experienced true, total loss, and had to rebuild his life knowing he'd never see Agnes again.

Dave wasn't dead. And Ellie was more afraid of having to see him again than not.

'We'll pass some interesting places on the way though,' he promised. 'Just watch.'

And she did. Maybe she was just too tired to object, or perhaps it was a convenient way to avoid more awkward conversation—Ellie honestly wasn't sure. All she knew was that her brain took the instruction and ran with it.

She leaned back in the comfortable padded seat of Jesper's car and rested her aching head as she stared out of the window. Yes, maybe this was craziness, but there was something calming about watching the snowy Danish countryside speed by outside, while the thrum of the engine and the warmth of the car lulled her into a sort of peace. For once, she didn't even feel the need to think—to plan, to strategize, to figure out what was next or what she was going to say to her mother or her agent next time they called.

She just…was.

After a long while of travelling in silence, Jesper's rumbling voice filled the car. 'If you're sleeping, you might want to wake up and open your eyes for the next bit.'

'I'm not sleeping,' Ellie said automatically, even though, actually, she wasn't sure. Her eyes felt heavy and gritty, and her mouth was dry. Maybe she'd dropped off. She hoped she hadn't been snoring.

She blinked a few times, then focused in on the view out of the window. 'What is *that*?'

'That is the Great Belt Bridge. Fourth longest suspension bridge in the world.' Jesper sounded personally proud of this Danish achievement. 'It means we can cross from Zealand—the island Copenhagen sits on—to Fyn and then on to the Danish mainland in practically no time at all.'

Ellie wasn't sure that bridges automatically led to national happiness, but she was willing to concede that it was quite the sight. And actually, now she thought about it, being able to get around a country easily and quickly had to be a plus, right? She still had occasional nightmares about being stuck in Crewe station in the freezing cold, having missed a connecting train back to London on her way home from university.

This bridge had the high concrete pylons and massive cables that spoke of solid and reliable engineering and, from what she could see, it was in heavy use.

'Is that a lighthouse?' Ellie peered out of the window at a small island that seemed to link one part of the bridge with another.

'That's the island of Sprogø,' Jesper replied without looking. 'There's a rail link as well as the road bridge from there, in the tunnels.'

'So, good transport infrastructure,' Ellie said. 'Road to happiness?'

He laughed. 'Could be. You're writing a social media post in your head already, aren't you?'

Rather than deny it, Ellie just opened the camera on her phone and snapped a few photos of the bridge and the lighthouse to post as a sort of immediate travel log with minimal commentary. She'd do a fuller, more reflective post later.

'You really are desperate to find the deep truth of happiness to share with your followers.' Jesper sounded slightly pitying, which instantly put her hackles up.

'I'm desperate not to have to pay back my advance to my publisher,' she countered. 'We can't all afford to go off-grid and search for our bliss for a couple of years. Some of us are on a budget and a timetable.'

He glanced across at her for just a second, before fixing his gaze firmly back on the road again. 'That's fair enough.'

They crossed the rest of the bridge in silence.

They arrived at his home in north Jutland late in the afternoon, just as the sun was slipping down over the horizon again. Ellie had slept for much of the drive, reducing the need for conversation, and Jesper had found himself strangely grateful for the solitude.

Or maybe not strangely. He was more used to being alone than in company these days, anyway.

And he didn't *understand* Ellie. He'd thought he did, when he'd offered to help her. He'd assumed she was a happiness tourist, fresh from a divorce, looking for life hacks to find her joy. He'd thought that he could show her a bit of Denmark and help her realise that true happiness went deeper than that. He'd believed this could be a fun, friendly jaunt to give his vague wanderings some purpose for the next few weeks, while he figured out what he was going to do next in his life. Something between the all and the nothing of his workaholic days and his stint in the wilderness.

Then, last night, he'd pulled out his laptop and searched for Ellie Peters online.

He'd found her social media instantly, before her website even, and been sucked in against his will. He wasn't a social media addict—avoided it like the plague if he could. Partly because he was certain that he was a happier person without it, but mostly because it was full of people who'd known him and Agnes before, and expected him to be the same person.

He couldn't be that person any longer. Couldn't fake it, even online to people he'd gone to primary school with. And he didn't feel comfortable showing them who he was now either.

Ellie, however, didn't seem to have any problem with being a completely different person online.

It had taken him a few moments to be sure he was even looking at the right person. Yes, there was the same hair, same eyes, same smile—except the smile looked less guarded in photos than in real life, and her eyes sparkled in a way he'd never seen.

There were shots and selfies from the night they'd met, taken at the Tivoli Gardens—fireworks and hot, greasy food and crowds and smiles. None of him, he noticed gratefully, but one of Ellie and Lily with their heads pressed together, smiling broadly.

Intrigued, he'd read the caption below, where Ellie had waxed lyrical about the power of a new year, the opportunities ahead, how she was excited to see where it led her. How her happiness quest had brought her experiences she'd never dreamed of, and so on.

None of which gelled with the frustrated author with writer's block—and happiness block—he'd shared pastries with in the café and promised to try to help.

Now, as he pulled his car to a stop in front of his seafront home, he looked over at the sleeping Ellie and wondered which was really the true woman, and which was the fake. He *thought* that the woman he'd been getting to know was the real thing—and, in truth, it seemed far more likely than the beaming, happy woman in the photos online.

Maybe nobody was really who they said they were any more.

But he found that he wanted to know more. To understand why and how she preserved this fake persona. What it gave her. What it achieved.

Who she really was underneath it all. Because if that Ellie wasn't real, maybe the one he'd met wasn't either. Maybe the truth was a different woman altogether.

Would he get to meet her during this happiness experiment? He hoped so.

As the engine cut out, Ellie stirred in the seat beside him. 'We're here?' Her voice was fuzzy with sleep and she blinked up at him adorably as she tried to focus. Here, again, was that different Ellie. Neither the beaming social media presence or the focused journalist he'd made his deal with. Just a woman waking up.

How long had it been since he'd watched a woman waking? Had he *ever*? He'd always been an early riser, and Agnes had liked to sleep in. He'd usually been in the office before she awoke, when they were married. Her days had been rather more…relaxed than his own, despite all the committees and boards she'd sat on.

'We're here,' he confirmed, his own voice a little gruff from misuse. 'Come on; I'll show you around and then we can bring the bags in.'

She nodded and fumbled for her seatbelt release. Jesper gritted his teeth to stop himself reaching to do it for her, and got out of the car.

She was his guest, not his lover. They'd agreed to be friends and nothing more. He was a teacher in this situation even—anything else would be a gross abuse of power.

But knowing that didn't seem to stop him wanting to know her better as a person. To lean in and help her with her seatbelt. To tuck her hair behind her ears and smile at her, maybe even steal another kiss.

Which was going to be a problem if he couldn't push those thoughts aside. Ellie had made it very clear that wasn't what she wanted from him, and he intended to make sure she never suspected he'd wanted it in the first place, in case it made her uncomfortable.

He just wasn't entirely sure how he was going to do that yet.

His housekeeper had been by that afternoon to air the place out, change the sheets and stock the fridge; her message to say that all was ready for them had buzzed through on his phone while he'd been driving. She'd left the lights on, too, so his home looked bright and welcoming against the darkening sky and the dramatic coastline beyond.

Jesper was surprised to feel a warmth of homecoming as he stepped up the path to the front door. He hadn't owned this place for more than a few years, and he'd spent most of his time there dragging himself out of the deepest despair. He'd always planned to sell it once he had himself back together again and move back to the city, or at least somewhere with another house within shouting distance.

But he hadn't. And now he wasn't even sure if he would. This place was his refuge, and he found himself reluctant to part with that.

'When you said you had a little place by the beach…this isn't exactly what I was expecting.' Ellie's tone was dry, but not disapproving.

He tried to look at the place through her eyes. He supposed it was a little larger than a beach house—he'd certainly found himself rattling around in there when he'd first moved in, unsure how to use all that space for one person. After a while, when he was feeling a little more stable, he'd got an interior designer in to sort the place out, while he was off somewhere else on a retreat. He'd left an empty shell and returned to a home, which had been a blessing he'd felt utterly unworthy of at the time, but now appreciated beyond measure.

'Come and take a look inside.' He held a hand out to her automatically, a misplaced reflex he couldn't bring himself to regret when she actually took it, her smooth palm and fingers cool in his. 'Welcome to my home,' he said, and meant it.

CHAPTER FIVE

WHEN JESPER HAD talked about his beach house, Ellie had imagined something like a small summer home, cabin-like even, perhaps. Instead, he'd brought her to a Scandi mansion by the sea.

The place was huge, that was a given. But it was also beautiful. Clean lines and pale, natural materials outside, blending in while also, somehow, standing out against the rugged coastline of northern Jutland. Its black roof spoke of stormy skies, while the pale wood walls echoed the sand she couldn't quite see over the green hills.

The lights were on inside, a beacon welcoming them home. Jesper led her through the dark front door, only dropping her hand once the door had shut behind them. She wasn't even sure why she'd taken his hand—or why he'd offered it. She wasn't a child, needing to be led. And she wasn't a date either—they'd both made that very clear.

But it had felt right. And now he'd let go... she missed the comforting warmth of his hand in hers.

Ellie shoved her hands in her pockets and looked around.

Inside, an open-plan living space spread all the way from the door to the huge windows that filled almost entire walls, looking out over the darkened beach, out to the sea. Any walls that weren't made of glass were either a soothing off-white colour or natural brick, and there was a wood-burning stove in the fireplace that kept the whole huge space toasty warm.

The living space was split into a large sitting area with a comfortable-looking dark grey corner sofa and a coffee table loaded with oversized books and magazines; a high-end kitchen with soft grey cabinets and wooden surfaces, with a long counter with stools that looked out over the dining area next door. A huge dining table filled that space, near one of the window walls, and it was fully set with eight places.

'Are we expecting company?' Ellie gestured to the dining table with its leafy green centrepiece in a wooden vase and the stacked plates on each of the woven willow placemats.

Jesper laughed. 'My housekeeper lives in hope.

She's probably stocked the fridge with enough food for an army.'

At the very mention of food, Ellie's stomach rumbled—and she realised what a long time ago the sandwiches they'd stopped for on the road had been.

He gave her a grin and a knowing look. 'Come on. Let me show you to your room, then I'll grab our stuff and make us some dinner.'

Her room—one of four guest rooms, as far as Ellie could tell—was beautiful. Simply but expensively furnished, with a huge bed covered with white linen and a soft sage-coloured headrest and a small wooden bedside table. The wooden floors were warm—underfloor heating, she supposed—and a floor-to-ceiling window on one side of the bed gave her what she was sure would be a magnificent view in the daytime.

She poked her head into the en suite bathroom while Jesper fetched her bag from the car and saw the most luxurious bathtub she could have ever imagined, as well as a large walk-in shower.

Yes, if she was looking for a place to find true happiness, she could have done a lot worse. Even the company was pretty good, she thought as Jesper dropped off her bags with another one of those enigmatic smiles that warmed her middle more than the underfloor heating did her toes.

Leaving unpacking for later, Ellie wandered through to the main living area again in time to see Jesper pulling out some wonderfully fresh-looking vegetables and other food from the fridge.

'Is pasta okay?' he asked without looking up. 'I figure it's quick and easy and we're both hungry.'

'Sounds perfect.'

He glanced up and smiled. 'Then take a seat, and I'll let you know when it's ready.'

Ellie nodded then moved away, towards the living area. But then she spotted the window seat—a long, cushioned bench set against one of those huge windows looking out over the beach. Grabbing a magazine from the coffee table, she curled herself up on it and made herself at home.

The magazine was in Danish, but that didn't matter since she only really wanted to look at the pictures. It was some sort of home and lifestyle glossy mag, with photos of perfect-looking Danish homes much like Jesper's, and perfectly styled dishes that made her stomach rumble again. Just leafing through it reminded her of the career and the life she'd left behind in London and, after a few minutes, she closed it again and stared out of the window instead.

She could hear the sea, she realised. The dull roar of the waves as they rushed forward and then pulled back, the rattle of the stones and sand as they were tossed in the water. The winter wind, as it whipped by them. The beach house was so well constructed and insulated that she hadn't noticed it at all anywhere else. But here, even by the obviously thick and double-glazed window, she could just make it out.

It awakened a sort of longing in her that she hadn't expected. She just couldn't quite identify what it was a longing *for*.

What did the sea tend to signify? Escape? Change? She wasn't sure.

She still hadn't figured it out by the time that Jesper called her over for dinner, but she was still pondering the question as she blew across the pasta and sauce before taking her first mouthful.

'This is delicious,' she told him, after she'd tasted it. 'Do you enjoy cooking, then?' Simple, easy, getting-to-know-each-other questions. That was what she needed to feel more on an even keel here. The problem was she'd gone too far, too fast—in fact she'd done almost everything so far in the wrong order.

She'd kissed him, then had deep conversations about happiness, and only *now* was she learning about his hobbies.

'I never used to,' Jesper admitted. 'Agnes and I...in New York we mostly survived on takeout, restaurant meals and leftovers. But when I moved back here...it's not so easy to find someone willing to deliver a pizza to the middle of nowhere. And, besides, I didn't want to see anyone, not even delivery drivers, for a while. So I taught myself to make some healthy, simple dishes, mostly so I wouldn't starve.'

'Well, it worked out well for me,' Ellie said with a smile, before taking another mouthful of the creamy pasta and sauce.

They ate the rest of the meal in a silence that started out comfortably but grew more awkward as it stretched out, filling the huge open-plan room. It lasted through the loading of the dishwasher, interrupted only by polite commentary and instructions. Ellie was about to yawn pointedly, maybe even with a little stretch, and make an excuse to disappear for an early night—even though she'd slept in the car—before Jesper cleared his throat and said, 'Would you like to take a walk on the beach before we turn in for the night? I always think the moon on the sea is the most beautiful thing about this place.'

And how could she possibly say no to that?

Jesper hadn't intended his suggestion to be romantic—in fact, he'd been trying to find anything that distracted him from the fact that he was staying in his remote beach house with a woman he found both attractive and intriguing, with no hope of doing anything at all romantic about it.

Which he knew, objectively, was for the best—he wasn't in a place to be pursuing romantic interests still, and he'd promised himself he'd keep things on an even, safe keel. Lust was the opposite of even.

Still, now they were strolling along the winter beachscape, wrapped up in warm coats and scarves wrapped around their necks, Jesper had to admit that there was at least a romantic edge to the outing.

From the way Ellie was keeping a careful one metre distance between them, he suspected that she had noticed it too. He tried to think of a way to explain what he'd really been thinking, bringing her out there. The last thing he wanted was for her to regret coming with him because she thought he was going to spend the whole time hitting on her.

He wasn't. No matter how tempting that idea was—because it was only really tempting if she reciprocated, and she'd already told him she wouldn't.

'Winter swimming is a big thing here in Denmark,' he said eventually. 'Going from the cold water to the sauna and vice versa especially.'

'You think I should go swimming in this sea?' Ellie sounded sceptical. He didn't blame her. The night was so black it was hard to tell where the beach ended and the water began.

'Well, not now,' he allowed. 'But before you leave, perhaps.'

'Maybe.' She eyed the waterline uncertainly. 'I know wild swimming has really taken off in the UK too, but I haven't tried it. Yet. But people say it does incredible things for their wellbeing in all sorts of ways.'

Jesper shrugged, hands safely in his pockets. 'Water has always been said to have healing properties, I suppose. And we're, what—eighty per cent water? Makes sense that we'd want to go back to it.'

'Hmm.' This time, she sounded rather more like she was considering the idea, which Jesper decided meant his work was done for the evening. All he'd promised to do was introduce her to things that might spark happiness. The sea, for him, was one of them.

He made a mental note of a few other water-based places they could visit as he continued walking—which meant it took a moment or two for him to realise that she wasn't following.

When he turned back, he found her standing a little closer to the shoreline, phone in hand as she photographed the moon's reflection shimmering on the waves.

'Sorry,' she said sheepishly when she was done. 'I realised I'd need a new image for tomorrow's social media posts and, well, this looked perfect. I might use a few of your house while I'm here too, if that's okay? I'll make sure they're all just glimpses and don't give away where we are—or show you at all. I know you value your privacy.'

'I do,' he replied. 'But I'm sure some carefully curated photos will be fine.'

They turned to continue their walk, but the interlude had given him exactly the opening he'd been looking for since he'd stumbled over her online presence the night before.

'I have to admit, I checked out your social

media accounts last night. You have a lot of followers.'

Ellie looked momentarily taken aback, but recovered quickly. 'I suppose that makes sense. I mean, you've invited a stranger into your home. Of course you'd want to know a little more about her. Me, I mean.'

'That was part of it, yes. But also… I wanted to know more about your quest for happiness.' He didn't mention that he'd felt like he knew her *less* after reading her online posts than he had after they'd spent New Year's Eve together.

'And what did you think?' Ellie asked. 'Like you said, I have a lot of followers. They expect a certain kind of content from me, so I try to live up to that.'

'It was all very well written, and the photos were beautiful.'

He could have left it there. He didn't have to say any more really, did he?

But Ellie gave him a knowing look and prompted, 'But?'

'It just didn't feel very like you, if I'm being honest.' He winced a little in anticipation of her response.

Luckily, Ellie didn't look offended at his observation. In fact, she laughed.

'Well, no. It's not me. It's the me that I'm

comfortable putting out there for others to meet.'

'That makes sense, I suppose.' Jesper shrugged. 'I guess I was just...surprised. Social media always feels like a game for teenagers or terrifyingly confident young adults to me.'

'I think it still is, in lots of ways,' Ellie admitted. 'Certainly, I think they are the ones who are comfortable putting their whole selves on show, the way their audience demands. But there's a place for us *older* contributors too, you know.'

'I wasn't saying you were old,' he said quickly.

Her laugh seemed to carry and crash onto the waves, breaking into melodic shards of echoes. 'I know that. And I understand what you're saying. But these days? Online is one of the only ways we have left to reach a larger audience, assuming you don't have the megabucks of the big companies. It's much more targeted, too. It's the great equaliser in some ways—and it means I can reach women just like me, or ones who want to read about the things I'm writing about. I'm not on there giving make-up tips or what have you. I'm writing exactly the same way I write in my book, so that when it's published they'll already know if they like it or not.'

He nodded. 'I can understand that. Except... you're *not* writing the book, but you *are* writing your social media posts. Why is that, do you think?'

Ellie pulled a face—one he could only just make out in the moonlight but made him laugh all the same.

'Isn't that the million-dollar question?' She sighed. 'I don't know. It's easy enough to keep up the facade when I'm writing online, but the moment I try to create something more...real, I suppose, it all dries up.'

Jesper considered the question. It seemed to him there was a fairly simple explanation, although he wasn't sure how well she'd take the suggestion. And really, what did he know of writing books? But if she could write one thing and not another...

'You might as well say it, you know,' Ellie said. 'Whatever it is you're thinking, I mean. We're stuck together now for the next few weeks. Might as well be honest with each other while we're at it. How am I supposed to learn about your happiness quest otherwise?'

He weighed up for a moment if she really meant it, and decided that she did. It was a question he'd had to ask himself often with his late wife, and one he'd regularly answered wrongly. But Ellie was watching him with wide, waiting eyes, as though she'd welcome whatever answer he had to give.

He supposed it didn't really matter what he thought anyway, which maybe made it easier to hear.

'I was just thinking that…maybe you find it harder to write the book because those pages are where you are truly yourself. Perhaps it is easier to put on a mask for others than to examine the truth in yourself. Being true to yourself, I have found, is an important part of happiness.'

Ellie's smile was somehow sad in the moonlight. 'You're probably right. But I'm not sure I've ever met anyone who is truly, completely themselves—and honest with themselves about it, too.'

'You've met me now,' he countered.

Her gaze turned speculative. 'Yes, I have. And do you honestly believe that you are true to yourself, and truthful *about* yourself, all the time?'

Did he? He'd thought that was what he'd been doing out here in the back of beyond all this time—finding his true core self and learning what made it tick, what he needed to survive and thrive in this world.

To be happy, but in a way that meant he'd dragged himself out of the pit of despair Agnes' death had put him in. The sense of his utter, utter failure that had led to it.

But now, with Ellie watching him so closely, waiting for his answer, he wondered if he'd really ever reached that level of truth.

I never told anyone about Agnes being pregnant when she died. Not even Will. And I never told them she was leaving me either.

Could he really claim to be truthful with himself, to be his *true* self as he was accusing her of not being online, if he still held those secrets so close to his chest?

'Maybe it's a work in progress for all of us,' he said finally, and she nodded her agreement.

'Well, perhaps I can get better at it during our trip.' Ellie tucked a hand through the crook of his elbow, the same way they'd walked together at the Tivoli Gardens on New Year's Eve. 'Perhaps we both can.'

'Perhaps.' Jesper couldn't shake the discomfited feeling her words left inside him, though. He'd brought her here to help her, to teach her, to show her all he'd learned.

He hadn't considered that she might have anything to teach him, too.

Or that he might have even been wrong about how far he'd come.

She shivered, and he turned them around, spinning past the shining sea to head back the way they'd come.

'Come on,' he said. 'Let's get back to the house. I've got a big day planned for us tomorrow.'

He'd show her the first places that he'd visited on his happiness quest. That would help him feel more in control of this situation.

He hoped.

'So, where are we going?' Ellie asked as Jesper's car pulled away from the beach house.

To be honest, she'd been reluctant to get back into the car after yesterday's long drive, but Jesper had promised her it would be worth it. He'd filled her in on his plans for the day over a simple breakfast of fruit and pastries, and excellent coffee. But it was only now she realised that, while he'd told her how long it would take to get there, what sort of footwear and layers to wear and where they'd stop for lunch, he hadn't actually told her where they would be going.

Jesper flashed her a quick smile. He seemed much more playful than he had on their pensive moonlight walk the night before. At moments, she'd felt he was almost nervous around her, keeping a safe distance away in case she got any ideas about this being anything more than an educational trip—which she definitely wasn't. And after their rather deep conversation about truth and reality online, he'd been keen to call it a night early—leaving her to enjoy the delights of the huge bathtub in her en suite bathroom before bed.

The relaxing water and bubbles hadn't stopped her thinking, though. Reflecting on everything Jesper had said about authenticity and being her true self. Although, if she was honest, she was more interested in what *he'd* been thinking about when he'd gone all quiet and decided it was time to return to the house and their separate rooms. Was there something he wasn't being honest with himself about? She thought there might be.

And, if she was being totally honest with *her*self, she had to admit that the part she was lying about most, even in her head, right now, had nothing to do with the book she hadn't written, or who she was online.

No, she was mostly lying to herself about how much she wanted to kiss Jesper again. As in she kept telling herself she didn't.

But she really, really did.

She sneaked a sideways look at him as he headed back out onto the main road. He was still smiling, his face handsome and just a little bit rugged in the weak winter sunshine, the silver at his temples sparkling.

'No, really. Where are we going?' She wasn't good with ambiguity. She needed to know the plan—and she had a horrible feeling that part of Jesper's quest for joy and authenticity involved throwing out the map and the plan and taking life as it came.

She'd never been very good at that.

'We're going to visit a church,' he said finally, still smiling as if he knew something she didn't. Which he did.

'A church?' She wasn't exactly a religious person. High days and holidays, weddings and christenings, that had been about it in her family—and less after her grandma had died. If Jesper thought she was going to find her true, authentic happiness and write about it through finding religion, he—and her publisher—were going to be disappointed.

Lily would have mentioned if he was a religious nut, right? One of those people who cults sent out to lure new people in—lost, hopeless people like her? The sort of cult that had nothing to do with real religion, or the nice church down the road that held jumble sales once a season, and more to do with crazed obsessiveness and sometimes mass suicide?

'Are we going to be…meeting any other people at this church?' she asked carefully, suddenly apprehensive.

He rolled his eyes. 'Your distrust of other people, and your conviction that happiness is something you can only find solo, is only going to make things harder, you know.'

Well, Lily had said the Danes could be blunt. So could she. 'Is that a yes?'

Jesper sighed. 'No, Lily, we will not be meeting any church members or cult-like figures today—that's what you're worrying about, right? I can't promise that there won't be any other people there, though. This particular church is quite a popular tourist attraction around Skagen.'

Skagen. That was right up at the tip of Denmark, she thought she remembered from the map she'd studied before her visit. 'I've never been to Skagen.' She admitted it as sort of a peace offering—an apology for believing, even for a moment, that he was about to kidnap her into a cult.

'It was the first place I went, after I moved

back to Denmark and bought the beach house.'
Jesper didn't sound offended by her assump-
tions, so hopefully that meant he'd forgiven her.
'I just got in the car one morning and drove,
heading to the edge of the world—well, the
country—to see what I found there.'

'And you found a church.' Ellie knew she
still sounded sceptical. She couldn't help it.

'I found a church,' he agreed. 'And now, so
will you.'

The drive wasn't too far and, less than an
hour later, Jesper pulled into a car park that was
already populated by at least a few other cars.

'I don't see a church,' Ellie said.

'This way.' He tucked her hand through
the crook of his arm, just as she had done last
night, and led her the way he wanted to go.

Ellie blinked as the church came into sight,
not entirely sure of what she was seeing. 'That's
the church?'

'What's left of it.' Jesper was smiling far
too broadly now, obviously enjoying his joke.
'Everything except the tower got buried under
the sand by shifting dunes, over two hundred
years ago.'

Ellie pulled away from him to explore closer.
It was the strangest sight: a bright white church
tower with a darker brown roof, poking out of

the green grasses and purple heather of the dunes that had swallowed it.

'Back when it was built, in the fourteenth century, it was one of the largest churches in the area. Vastly wealthy, big congregation, you know. Important.' Jesper's voice was soft as he told her the history of the place. 'Then the sands came and in no time it was gone. Stripped of anything of value, and all that remained was this.'

'Oh.' The sound she made was involuntary, an exclamation of understanding more than anything.

Now she saw why he'd brought her here.

He was the church. She knew how rich and successful he'd been over in the States, before his wife's death. The event, like those shifting sands, that had changed his fortunes overnight.

But he'd dug himself out, hadn't he? He wasn't still buried in the sands like the church was.

Like she was, if she was honest with herself. Burying herself, or her head at least, in the sand and pretending that Dave and Maisie's wedding wasn't happening. That her career wasn't on the verge of collapsing.

'What does it make you think about?' Jesper's voice was suddenly very close, and she realised he was standing directly behind her. She wondered if she'd looked wobbly as her revelations had crashed over her, and he'd been making sure he was close enough to catch her if she fainted or fell.

She had to admit, her legs felt less stable than they had.

'It makes me think…that nothing stays the same,' she said slowly. 'That even strong, stable, eternal things can crumble or be swallowed up. That change always happens, and all we can do is work with it.'

He nodded. 'That's what it makes me think, too. And, you know, this church is now a popular tourist attraction—probably more popular than it would have been if it had stayed as a church. In the summer, you can even buy tickets to go inside the tower, and there's a kiosk selling ice cream and all sorts.'

Even after disaster had struck, after the church had been buried and could have just been left to decay and fade away…it had found a new life as something else.

Ellie smiled up at him. 'I like that idea.'

'Me too.' He reached over to squeeze her shoulder. 'Come on. I've got plenty more to show you.'

'Where are we going next?' she asked as they headed for the car.

'Somewhere else with another message for us.'

CHAPTER SIX

JESPER FELL BACK and watched as Ellie stood at the very tip of Jutland, watching the ever-changing line in the waves where two seas met and merged. He couldn't see her face, but he could imagine the look of wonder he was sure was there. Even from behind, he could make out her hands, held at her sides but with the fingers taut and stretched, as if she was holding herself back from touching the water.

If it had been summer, he was sure she'd have her shoes off and be ankle-deep in the waves already. The currents were too strong to allow for sea-bathing, but there was still something magical about being at the point where two worlds collided—and a person could see it happening.

He'd been pleased—and silently relieved— that she'd understood the message he'd found in the church, and his reasons for taking her there. None of the metaphors for change and growth he'd come across on his 'quest' as she called it had been particularly subtle, but then, in Jesper's experience, once he'd started looking, almost *everything* he came across had a message for him.

Maybe it was more about the recipient than the message. In which case, he hoped that Ellie was as open to receiving them as he had been.

What was she thinking right now? She'd been standing there, staring at the waves, for ages now.

Jesper had never claimed to be a particularly patient man.

'What do you think?' he asked, raising his voice a little so she could hear him over the waves.

Ellie didn't turn around as she responded. 'I think it's wonderful. Two worlds colliding.'

Hearing her echo his own thoughts only confirmed to him that he'd been right to bring her here. She needed this.

She hadn't confessed all her reasons for coming to Denmark, he was sure of it. But he sensed that she was at a crossroads, much as he had been when he'd first come to this spot. He hoped it would help her make sense of the world, the same way it had him.

'It's like…it's like a sliding doors moment

somehow,' Ellie went on, almost as if she were talking to herself and not him. 'I'm at a place where two seas meet, and I have to decide which one I'm going to sail and leave the other sea, the other life, behind.' She shook her head. 'Listen to me, I sound ridiculous—like I'm about to take up a life of piracy.'

'No. You don't.' He stepped closer, until he stood almost beside her on that tip of land that marked the end of Denmark and the start of whatever came next, listening to the waves and watching the warring water where it met. 'I felt exactly the same when I came here for the first time. Like I was choosing which future I wanted. Which way to go next.'

He'd thought, back then, that he'd made the decision. That he knew where his life was going.

Coming back here with Ellie, though… Jesper found himself staring out at the waters, wondering if he was at another turning point. Another moment in his life when two possible paths were separating out in front of him and, sooner or later, he was going to have to decide which one to walk.

He'd let people back in. First Will, and Anders and Lily. Now Ellie.

Sure, none of them were Agnes. There wasn't

the heavy responsibility of a marriage he couldn't make work, couldn't dedicate himself to. The expectations he couldn't live up to—because, God knew, Agnes had expected a lot, but that was what he'd signed up for, and in the end he'd been found wanting.

But they were people, all the same. People he cared about and, in Ellie's case, someone he found himself drawn to know better. To understand.

And however much he lied to himself about it, however careful he was to respect her space and keep his distance…in his heart he knew he wanted to kiss her again. Had wanted it ever since the moment their lips had separated on New Year's Eve.

Was that why he was doing this? Out of a misguided hope that it might get him into her bed?

He hoped not. He hoped he was a better person than that. He'd worked hard to be, these past few years.

No, he was doing this for her, to help her find happiness. And if it gave him a sense of purpose for a few weeks that was an added bonus. This was about her, not him.

But she was showing him a life where he didn't have to be alone for ever. The one thing he hadn't contemplated after Agnes' death—the idea of finding, well, love again.

He didn't love Ellie. He barely knew her.

But he couldn't shake the feeling that he *could* love her, if he let himself. If she let him.

A cold, sharp wind blew across them and Ellie shivered, huddling back into her coat. Jesper moved instinctively closer, then stopped himself before he touched her. What was he going to do? Wrap his arms around her? Warm her with his body heat?

That didn't sound like something just friends did, and she'd been very clear that was all they ever could be.

Besides, on the wind he could hear his personal demons whispering, reminding him what happened when he felt too much, when he moved to the extremes—of work, of love, of life.

The extremes were where everything fell apart. Go too far one way, and everything else would be ripped away from him.

The extremes got people killed, and he couldn't lose another person.

Even if, in his more rational moments, he knew that the universe didn't really operate that way, that Agnes hadn't died because he'd worked too much, it didn't change the fundamentals.

If he hadn't been obsessed with his work, too busy to pay her the attention she'd needed, to love her the way she'd wanted, to live the life she'd married him for, then she would never have been on her way to the airport in the first place. She'd never have been in that car crash, and she wouldn't have died, taking their unborn child with her.

If he had been enough, Agnes would still be alive.

Jesper stepped back. 'We should get going.'

Ellie nodded and turned away from the waves, casting one last look over her shoulder at the place where two seas met as she headed for the car.

He followed more slowly, still thinking.

Yes. The extremes got people killed.

And love was about as extreme as life got, wasn't it?

It wasn't a risk he could take.

They headed into the town of Skagen proper, with its golden houses and red roofs, somehow sunshiny and hopeful even in the depth of winter. The seaside town was beautiful, the museum they toured fascinating and the harbour atmospheric. The café they stopped at for a late lunch was inviting and cosy and the freshly caught seafood delicious.

But Ellie knew she wasn't paying full attention to any of it. Whatever lesson Jesper thought that Skagen had to offer, she was missing it. Because she was still hung up on the last one.

That incredible sight of two seas meeting, washing up over each other, fighting for dominance and retreating again, away from the spit of land where they clashed. She'd never seen anything like it.

She wondered what Jesper had seen there, the first time he'd visited. The message it had for him. He'd said it was the same as hers, but she could sense that there was something he was holding back. But what? He'd already told her his story—the tragic death of his wife, and his retreat from the world until he'd found a way to exist in it again.

What more could there be?

But then, he probably thought she'd told him her whole story, too.

'Time to head back to the beach house?' she asked as he waved away her offer to split the bill. She'd feel worse about that if Lily hadn't told her he was richer than God. 'The sun will be going down soon.'

He flashed her a sudden smile. 'Exactly. Which means we've got one more thing to see.'

Ellie frowned as she tried to figure out what he was talking about, and quickly gave up. Jesper knew this place far better than she ever could and, given the wonders he'd shown her today—sights she'd never have thought to visit on her own—there was no point in even trying to guess.

It turned out to be another beach, of sorts, not too far away.

'This is Høgen—Old Skagen,' Jesper told her as they made their way towards what seemed to be a purpose-built viewing platform above the dunes. 'And this is Sunset Viewpoint. Come on.'

He reached out and took her hand, leading her towards a long, slatted wooden bench that undulated along its length like the sand dunes it sat beside. They took their seats, along with a few other couples—some older, some younger—and waited, and watched as the sun began to sink over the waves, turning the whole sky a fiery orange followed by a glowing pink.

She reached for her phone and snapped a couple of quick photos.

'It's beautiful,' Ellie admitted in a whisper. 'I assume there's another message here?'

'Of course,' he murmured, and she realised he was closer than she'd thought, his head bent near to hers to hear her speak. 'Can you guess what it is?'

Ellie stared out at the changing sky, the disappearing sun, going out in a blaze of glory even in the dull winter sky. It would stay down for long hours tonight, she knew. But it would be back again in the morning, ready to do this all over again tomorrow night.

Just like her, she supposed.

'When the sun goes down on one day, there's another one waiting to dawn?' she guessed. 'Very musical theatre of you, really.'

'Well, yes,' he admitted. 'But it also has the magic of being true. There's never yet been a sunset that didn't see a sunrise, too.'

'Unless you live right up at the tip of Finland or one of those places that doesn't get light at all in the winter,' she mused, mostly to rile him.

He rolled his eyes, close enough that she could see the amusement in them. 'I suppose.'

She nudged his shoulder with her own. 'I take your point though. One ending is always a beginning of something new.'

'Exactly. Knowing that, believing that...it

helped me a lot. I felt like my life had ended when Agnes died. The first thing I had to recognise was that it was the start of something new. Not something I wanted, or enjoyed, or looked forward to, not at first, and some days still not now. But it *was* new, and different. And that meant I could live it differently, too.'

Ellie nodded slowly, her mind turning his words over and over as she considered them. Moving on was hard at the best of times, and the death of a spouse was anything but that. She had to admire his ability to make that choice in the first place—and to share it with her, to help her do the same?

Jesper was a stronger man than she suspected he'd ever give himself credit for. And it stirred up all sorts of feelings inside her chest that she really wasn't ready for.

'You must still miss her terribly,' she said.

'I… I do,' he replied, but Ellie could sense a 'but' coming. 'We didn't…towards the end, we didn't spend much time together at all. I wasn't, well… I wasn't all she'd hoped for in a husband, I think. Know, really. I know I wasn't. So yes, I miss her. I miss what I thought our marriage could have been. I miss the woman I fell in love with. But some days…some days it feels like she's just in another room, another place, waiting for me to come home so she can tell me how I've let her down today.'

It wasn't what she'd expected. Without realising it, she'd painted a picture of the perfect marriage in her head, to explain the depth of his grief that had driven Jesper away from the world. But she knew herself that even the most perfect-seeming marriage had its cracks and fissures. Just look at her and Dave.

Her only failure, as far as she'd been able to ascertain, was not being twenty-two any longer.

She swallowed and looked away, eager to find a new subject. 'So, tomorrow's new dawn—what will that bring? What have you got planned for us next? Another message, I assume?'

'Of course.' Jesper sounded relieved to be back on topic, too. 'But I can't tell you what just yet.'

She jerked her head up to meet his gaze, only to discover that he was closer than ever. So close that, if she wanted, she could bring her lips to his with only the slightest movement.

If she wanted to.

Oh, God, she wanted to. However inappropriate it might be.

Her throat dry, she tried to swallow before she spoke. 'You can't tell me?'

He shook his head, bringing his face even closer to hers, the last of the sunlight shimmering off the silver in his beard. 'But I promise you it's magical.'

Magical.

That kiss at New Year had been magical—unexpected, with literal fireworks going off in the sky behind them. A gentle but all-encompassing kiss that had suddenly opened up a world or a future she hadn't even contemplated before. That kiss had been her sunken church finding a new lease of life, her oceans meeting and crashing, her sunset before the sunrise.

And she could have it again, if she just leant in one iota.

She couldn't breathe with wanting it.

Except…

Her new day couldn't be about some guy. Her joy, her future, had to be something she found in herself, not another person.

For too long, her husband had been her happiness—her marriage, her lifestyle, everything they had together had been what made her *her*. Ellie.

And she couldn't risk falling into that trap again.

She pulled away—but not fast enough to miss the spark of hurt in Jesper's eyes.

But then he gave her a small smile, got to his feet and held a hand out to pull her up.

'Come on. We should get back. Big plans tomorrow.'

'Right.'

Ellie followed him back to the car, still thinking.

She couldn't kiss him, and she'd told him why. But she hadn't told him everything.

If he knew about Dave and Maisie, if she told him the truth about why she was in Denmark, then he'd understand why she couldn't risk kissing him again.

She owed him that much.

She just needed to figure out how to do it.

'Thank you for this,' she said suddenly, before he could open the car door. 'Really. I think… I think today has given me at least part of what I was looking for. I think that maybe I can even start writing now.' She'd have to update her social media accounts before she looked at her manuscript, but for the first time in a long time she thought she could be honest there, too. Well, a *bit* more honest, anyway.

His smile was slow and warm and made her feel the same way the sunset had. 'I'm glad. But I promise you, we're only just getting started.'

He opened the door and climbed into the

driver's seat, which meant he didn't see her shiver.

Or hear her murmur, 'That's what I'm worried about.'

Ellie had something she wasn't telling him—Jesper was almost certain of it.

She was quiet on their return from Skagen, retreating into her bedroom at the beach house immediately after they'd shared a light supper—during which she was almost silent.

The next day he took her to the Troll Museum, and they laughed at the funny hair and odd expressions of the little creatures that were supposed to bring good luck, apparently.

'My dad used to have a whole collection of them,' Ellie said absently. But that was about the most she *did* say.

Oh, she took photos, of course, and uploaded them from her phone to her social media accounts while he watched, adding pithy commentary about their adventures. But he knew instinctively that those words didn't match her thoughts. She was being her online self again—just when he'd hoped she might have started being her real self a bit more.

'Did you like it?' he asked on their way back to the beach house.

'Well, you promised it would be magical,' Ellie replied. 'I suppose trolls count. Although when you said trolls I was sort of expecting, you know, full-sized monster ones.'

'These are cuter,' he said with a shrug. 'Did you get the message, though?'

He'd had to spend a little time thinking about what the message would actually be. He hadn't really planned out their itinerary for their time together, much as he might like to give the impression that he had. He was just retracing his steps from his own adventures. And the Troll Museum, while quirky, hadn't exactly been a planned stop for him. More somewhere he'd found himself unexpectedly while wandering. But he'd been charmed all the same.

He'd hoped Ellie would be, too.

She screwed up her nose as she thought about it.

'Um…that you have to lighten up and laugh at life sometimes?' she guessed. 'I mean, that's what I'll probably use in my round-up post tomorrow.'

He grinned at her. 'Yeah, that works.'

She stared at him for a moment, her mouth slightly open. 'You're making this up as you go along, aren't you?'

'Not all of it,' he protested. 'I just thought you'd like to see the trolls.'

She gave him a soft smile—one of those ones that made his heart start to ache. 'I did. Thank you.'

Still, when they got home to the beach house that evening, she pulled out her laptop and worked while he cooked dinner, and then she went to bed as soon as they'd finished clearing up. No more moonlight walks on the beach, and no more almost kisses like there had been in Skagen.

Was that why she seemed more distant? Was she *trying* to put space between them after that moment—that glorious moment when he'd thought, hoped, that she might be about to kiss him?

She hadn't, and he'd respected that. She didn't need to put space between them on his account.

Which meant she had to be doing it on hers. Because maybe she had wanted that kiss as much as he had.

And whatever her true reason for not trusting in the thing that was building between them— chemistry, connection, whatever she wanted to call it—Jesper was certain it was the reason she was hiding in her room every evening.

That there was something she wasn't telling him.

He'd never been good with secrecy either.

Luckily, he had plenty of opportunities to try and tease the truth out of her.

'If you're not going to try wild swimming in the sea—'

'In January, in Denmark,' she interrupted. 'No.'

'Then we'll just have to find a suitable alternative,' Jesper finished, casting her a smile.

She'd been suspicious when he'd insisted on her packing her swimming things for their latest day out—he could tell by the way her eyes had narrowed as she'd studied him, searching for nefarious intent. But when he'd promised she wouldn't be swimming in the freezing ocean, she'd finally agreed. That didn't mean she'd stopped asking questions, though.

In fact, she was still asking them right up until the moment he pulled up outside the most exclusive spa hotel in the region.

There were other, more famous spas in the country, and he'd considered taking her to all of them, but many of the best-known ones would be rife with tourists even in January, and besides, this was the spa he'd visited in his own quest for a new, content life, so it seemed right to bring Ellie there too.

The hotel building stretched out along a bank of green grass, pale stone topped by a red-tiled roof, and small windows with copper-green canopies. Another time, he thought he might have brought her here to stay the night, or longer, but that sort of thing suggested a more romantic purpose than Jesper had in mind.

Something he had to remind himself of after they'd checked in and separated to change into their swimwear. And when they met again, outside the thermal baths, and he got his first look at her in her swimsuit.

It wasn't as if it was anything particularly revealing or racy. Just a fairly standard-cut one-piece swimming costume in a dark forest-green. Perfectly ordinary. Except for one thing.

The zip that travelled up between her breasts to the V of the neckline. A zip that she could, at any time, just undo…but of course she didn't. Which didn't stop him from imagining it, all the same.

Ellie gave him a puzzled look. 'Everything okay?'

Jesper cleared his throat. 'Fine. Shall we… explore the spa?'

'Sounds like a plan.'

Together, they set off through the heated air, completing a full circuit of the facilities—from the thermal showers to the salt-water bath overlooking the forest, from the three different temperatures of sauna to the cold plunge pool just outside. They didn't have the spa to themselves, but at the same time it wasn't busy, which Jesper decided was probably the best combination. Alone, he might have been even more tempted by that bloody zip.

They completed their first circuit and decided to take a dip in the forest pool to acclimatise. Jesper hung back and watched as Ellie kicked off and covered the distance between the tiled steps and the far end of the pool in long, easy strokes.

When she paused, arms resting on the far edge, he followed.

'What do you think?' he asked as he drew level.

'It's amazing.' Ellie stared out at the wide, wide window surrounding the three sides of the pool that jutted out into the forest, almost as if they were swimming in a lake between the trees. Then she looked up at him with an impish smirk. 'Although I have to say I'm relieved that we're allowed to wear swimwear. I thought all your Danish spas and saunas required guests to be naked.'

He chuckled. 'Many of our saunas and spas *are* nude facilities, but I wasn't sure that would make you happy right now. And since that is the object of the exercise...'

'You're right.' She looked down at her body—lithe and lean with muscle, curving in absolutely all the right places, and with that damn zip hanging on by a thread. 'Maybe twenty years ago I'd have been game, but now...not so much.'

Jesper stared at her for a moment with a complete lack of comprehension.

'Clearly, you don't see what I see.' And it was probably only the heated air making his voice rough. Ellie looked up in surprise and he swallowed, forcing himself to look away. For him, she was far more gorgeous than any twenty-something. But he couldn't exactly say that when they had set their rules so carefully to ensure that they were only friends.

Something he perhaps should have thought more carefully about before planning to spend the day with her in nothing but that swimsuit.

Instead, he played a hunch and asked, 'What would you have done if it was a nude spa?'

Ellie laughed. 'I'd have been incredibly un-comfortable, I imagine.'

Jesper wasn't joking, though. 'But you'd have told me? You'd have refused to come in? I mean, if you were so uncomfortable, you wouldn't have stripped naked and come in any-way, just to avoid conflict?'

'No. I... I mean, I agreed to do whatever you suggested on this trip, to go where you wanted, so... I hope I'd have at least *mentioned* that I wasn't entirely comfortable with the idea.' She didn't even sound fully convinced of that much.

'You hope,' he repeated flatly.

Ellie pulled a face and spun around in the water, leaning back against the tiles and star-ing into the spa itself instead of out into the woods. 'I suppose... I've always been one to go along with what others expect of me. To not let them down more than to avoid conflict, I think. I want people to think well of me.'

'I hope you know that if I ever ask for some-thing you don't want to give, I'd always rather you say no than do something that makes you uncomfortable,' he said.

'I do,' she replied, her smile a little tight. 'Now, I'm going to take advantage of this beau-tiful pool for a while before you drag me into the sauna!'

She pushed away fast, her head in the water and her arms arcing out overhead as she sped away from him. Jesper watched her go, relieved that he wasn't going to be drawing her into anything she didn't want, but wishing he wasn't so sure that he was the only one in her life who wasn't.

The spa Jesper had chosen to bring her to was stunning, but Ellie had to admit that she wasn't entirely sure what the message was in it. When she asked him, over a delicious light lunch taken in fluffy white dressing gowns, he simply shrugged and said, 'Some days you need to let go and relax,' which Ellie wasn't sure was everything she was supposed to get from the experience.

Oh, but it felt good, though.

Just pushing her body through the water, feeling the movement, her progress, felt like a shift. Like she was making something happen, instead of letting life happen to her.

Even this happiness quest was being guided by Jesper—he was choosing where she went and when, what lessons she learned. But her own body was something she still had control over. And that gave her control too, if the way Jesper's eyes kept darting down to the zip closure of her swimming costume was anything to go by.

Eventually, she couldn't put off the sauna any longer.

'If you really hate it, you don't have to stay in,' Jesper said prosaically. 'And we'll start with the coolest one. Then, when you get too hot, you go out there and jump in the cold plunge pool.'

She shuddered at the very idea. 'No, thanks.'

Jesper held the sauna door open for her, heat radiating out. 'Don't knock it until you've tried it.'

Even the coolest sauna felt like the hottest summer's day she could remember, surrounding every inch of her. Jesper climbed up the wooden slats to sit on the very highest bench, while Ellie stayed further down. When he tipped his head back and closed his eyes, she couldn't quite resist taking a good, long look at him in his own swimming trunks, though.

She knew he had to be older than her, nearly fifty if he was the same age as Anders, but she wouldn't have guessed it otherwise. Despite the traumas and isolation of the last few years, he'd kept himself in great shape, with only the silvering hair giving away his age.

She made herself look away. Sweat was start-ing to drip down between her breasts from the sauna alone. She didn't need to make things worse by salivating over a man she'd already decided she couldn't have.

Still, by the time she'd stretched out and found a comfortable position on the lower, cooler bench, she was starting to wonder if he'd actually fallen asleep up there.

Until he said, 'So. Tell me about your husband.'

'Ex-husband,' she shot back, trying not to sound startled. 'Did Lily tell you I was divorced?'

'She did.' Jesper opened his eyes and peered down at her. 'But mostly I just learned about it from your social media. It seemed…amicable? Or was that just for the masses?'

'Why do you care?' She didn't mean it to come out as harsh as it sounded. It was probably the heat, going to her head.

He shrugged, and water droplets ran in rivulets down his torso. 'I care about helping you, about this quest we're on together. I'm trying to get a picture of the real you so I can help you best, but so far…it's hard to tell which is the real you and what's just a front you put on for your readers.'

That, as much as it pained her to admit it, was fair. 'It *was* amicable. We just…grew apart, I suppose. I mean…we were still teenagers when we met, at university. And nobody stays the same person their whole life, do they?'

'I suppose they don't.' The words sounded heavy in the thick, hot air. 'I know Agnes and I… I thought I knew who she wanted me to be, and I gave everything I had to be that person. But in the end, it wasn't enough to make her happy.'

Ellie's chest tightened at the sadness in his voice. This man who tried so hard—was trying so hard now, for her, just out of a new, budding feeling of friendship. It broke her heart that he felt he wasn't enough—and could never be now, for a wife who had died unsatisfied.

But then, she knew too how hard it was to know that there was nothing she could do or say to magically become what someone else wanted, no matter how hard she'd tried over the years to contort herself into the right shape, the perfect wife.

It wasn't as if she could wave a wand and become twenty years younger, after all.

'I know how that feels,' she said softly.

Jesper looked down, his gaze somehow hotter than the sauna air. 'He wanted you to be someone other than you are?' He shook his head. 'Then he's an idiot.'

Suddenly, the rising heat of the sauna was too much. 'I need to…' Ellie motioned vaguely towards the door and let herself out, and didn't even pause before sinking straight into the ice-cold plunge pool outside.

CHAPTER SEVEN

AFTER THEIR DAY at the spa, when he'd finally thought he was making some progress in getting Ellie to open up to him, Jesper was rather disappointed to discover that the next week progressed in much the same way as it had before. He'd make them breakfast—well, lay out whatever treats his housekeeper had left for them the previous day—and they'd drink coffee together, then they'd venture out into the wider world to see or experience something Danish and meaningful. Something he'd seen on his quest that had stuck with him.

Each evening, he'd check her social media to see what she'd had to say publicly about their adventures, and assess how it matched up with the experience as he'd lived it. He was pleased to see that at least the smiles in her selfies, and the comments underneath, were beginning to reflect the woman he was growing to know a little more every day.

He particularly liked the shot she'd taken from the spa pool, looking out at the forest from the water, with the caption, 'my new happy place'. It seemed his ill-thought-out and impulsive plan was working.

He never did manage to persuade her to try wild swimming, despite her sudden affinity for the icy plunge pool, and she laughed when he took her to Legoland, but was happy to find a message about play and creativity in there that he wasn't sure he'd have come up with on his own.

Every day they experienced something together and talked about it. Every day he felt a little bit closer to her, as if he understood her a little bit more, even if he knew there were still many things she didn't feel comfortable telling him, yet.

And every day he resisted the urge to kiss her when her eyes lit up and she talked about what she'd found in their day's adventures.

Then every evening they'd go back to the beach house and she'd curl up with her laptop, eat dinner and go to bed, without ever allowing that same closeness to penetrate the world they had in his home.

Was it because she was afraid they wouldn't be able to resist the attraction between them?

It was a reasonable fear, he supposed. But all he knew was that, once the sun went down, he felt her pull away from him. And it stung a little bit more every day.

After a week, he decided it was time to move on.

'Move on to where?' Ellie asked, in between packing up those belongings of hers that seemed to have migrated over every inch of his home.

He picked up a fluffy cardigan that had been left hung on the back of a dining chair and tossed it to her. 'Aarhus. Denmark's second city. Known as the city of smiles.'

He punctuated that knowledge with a smile of his own, pleased and relieved when she returned it.

'Where will we stay?'

'Will and Matthew have a penthouse apartment there that they rent out,' he explained. 'I asked them if we could use it for a few days.'

'A few days? Is there lots to see there?' She seemed intrigued at the idea.

'Plenty. And besides, I think…maybe you'll feel more comfortable in a city. Somewhere less remote.' Somewhere she could leave and get a hotel room if things started feeling too close, perhaps.

She gave him a puzzled look. 'Comfortable? I'm plenty comfortable here, you know. This place is like…extreme luxury to us mere mortals. You should have seen my flat in Copenhagen!'

'I didn't mean that kind of comfortable,' he said awkwardly. 'I just meant…it's only the two of us here, and don't think I haven't noticed the way you retreat to your room every time that's the case.'

She winced, and gave him an apologetic smile. 'That's not… I'm not uncomfortable. I just think it's for the best. I've got… I've got a lot on my mind.'

As if he hadn't noticed.

This was it, he realised. His best chance to ask her *what* exactly was on her mind. What she wasn't telling him.

So he took a breath, and said, 'Want to tell me about it?'

It was the perfect opportunity. The perfect moment to tell him everything—just like she'd been meaning to all week.

And yet, when she was presented with it… she bottled it.

'Nothing, really,' she said lightly. 'Um, things are just going really well with the book, finally.

No more blank pages—I'm making real progress! And that's all thanks to you, so…thank you.'

It was true, all of it. The document on her laptop was filling out with anecdotes and mini essays on their adventures—a mixture of travel writing and personal reflections, descriptions of the places they'd visited and accounts of the conversations they'd been having about happiness and messages along the way.

She genuinely felt she was learning what she needed to on this trip. Jesper had lived up to his promise and then some.

So yes, it was all true.

It just wasn't The Truth, with the capital letters.

Because the truth was that every place they went, every sight they saw together, every meal spent discussing the Danish way of life and how hard it had been to adjust back after life in the States, and how he'd just had to go cold turkey and not do *anything* for a while…every moment she spent with Jesper, she fell harder for him.

It wasn't even just the way she wanted to kiss him any more.

That first walk on the beach, or that day watching the sunset together, or yes, the day at the spa, kissing had been the main thing on her mind. She'd experienced his lips once and she'd like to do it again, please.

But, worse than that, she was starting to have *feelings* to go along with the wanting to kiss him. The sort of crush-like feelings she hadn't felt since before she was married. Since the early days after she'd met Dave, actually.

Which was the part that was freaking her out the most, she knew.

Oh, it wasn't as if she was falling madly in love with him and would be heartbroken when she left or anything. She'd only known the guy for a week or two, and she liked to think that she had more sense than *that*.

It was just…she could feel the potential humming underneath their every interaction.

They could be *magnificent* together. But if they were, that meant giving up her quest to find happiness on her own terms, without relying on somebody else to give it to her.

And she just couldn't do that.

Which was why she hadn't told him about Dave and Maisie getting married. Oh, she'd meant to—even started to a couple of times. But she knew that once all her dirty laundry was aired, and he understood the real reasons she was in Denmark, there was no going back from that.

What if he looked at her with pity? She couldn't stand that.

But worse…what if he understood, and convinced her that she could move on, could have something with him, and she believed him?

What if he broke down all her defences, and she fell?

Right now, her secrets and her early bedtimes were the only thing protecting her from screwing up this happiness book project. And, okay, fine, yes, also protecting her heart. Because she'd never been good at casual and carefree, and she was fairly sure Jesper hadn't either. They were the sort of people who felt things deeply.

And she couldn't risk feeling that way again. Not after what happened last time she fell.

Jesper watched her for a few more moments then, when it became clear she wasn't going to say anything more, gave a small nod. 'I'm really glad it's going well. The book, I mean.'

'Me too.' Ellie nodded and smiled and knew he was seeing right through it. He knew she wasn't saying something.

And she suspected he also knew that she couldn't keep silent for ever.

I'm going to have to tell him. But I'm going to have to protect my heart when I do.

Ellie was sad to leave the beach house; it had been a happy place for her, in a way that the apartment in Copenhagen never had been. But she was excited to explore Aarhus, too. On the drive, she used her phone to look up facts about Denmark's second city, relating them all to Jesper, who just nodded and said, 'I know,' to every one.

After he'd failed to be surprised by the information that the city had been founded by the Vikings in the eighth century, that the cathedral was the longest *and* tallest in Denmark, or that the Danish women's handball team had their headquarters in Aarhus, Ellie took to making up facts to see if she could catch him out.

'Oh, and the world's largest emerald was found there in 1789,' she said casually.

'I know.' Jesper's reply was automatic. Then he frowned. 'Wait. You made that one up.'

Ellie laughed. 'I wouldn't have to if you weren't such a know-it-all.'

'I lived in Aarhus once, when I was younger,' he said with a shrug. 'I know the place pretty well.'

She stared at him. 'You realise that if you'd

told me that sooner I wouldn't have spent the last half an hour trying to tell you about the place?'

'I liked listening to you,' he replied simply. 'It's nice to hear you excited about something.'

'Hmm.' Ellie returned to learning about Aarhus in silence. At least she might get some ideas about where he was likely to take her while they were there.

Knowledge was power, after all.

He'd really thought she was going to tell him the truth.

Instead, she'd prattled on about the book, then spent the whole drive to Aarhus telling him facts he already knew. Which, actually, he'd quite enjoyed, but that wasn't the point.

She wasn't telling him something. And the longer she went not telling him…the worse whatever the secret was became in his imagination.

He'd considered calling Lily and just begging for information, but just about managed to resist. Partly because it was a gross violation of Ellie's privacy, and mostly because she wouldn't tell him anyway.

She'd tell Ellie he'd been asking, though. Maybe that would prompt her to talk…

But not if it was really bad. Still, he was fairly sure that whatever she was keeping from him couldn't be as awful as the things he hadn't told her about his wife's death.

So maybe they would have to call it even.

Will and Matthew's flat in Aarhus was as splendid as he remembered, and Ellie's face lit up when she took in the luxurious accommodations. He knew she'd been sad to leave the beach house, but it seemed that a penthouse apartment looking out over Aarhus harbour made up for it.

They spent the first evening wandering around the city, stopping for drinks and dinner at bars and a restaurant that appealed to them from the street. It was still too cold to be outside for too long at night, but they'd wrapped up warm and besides, the chill gave him an excuse to take her arm and pull her close against him.

He kept her out late deliberately, so she couldn't escape to her room away from him too early. As a result, they talked and talked until way past her customary bedtime and, when they did make it back to the flat, Jesper fell into bed with a smile on his face.

Then he sat up again, and scrubbed a hand through his hair to bring him to his senses.

What was he doing?

He was grinning like a schoolboy after a first date with his high school crush, and they hadn't even *kissed* yet. Well, they hadn't kissed again, anyway. The closest they'd got that night was when she'd given him a hug goodnight, still wrapped up in jumpers and scarves and her coat, and pressed her cold lips against his cheek.

Was he really this happy at a kiss on the cheek?

Well, it seemed, yes, he was.

God, he was in trouble.

But he was still smiling when he fell asleep.

The next day, he took Ellie to the ARoS Art Museum.

'The place with the rainbow panorama?' she asked, bouncing on her toes a little as they walked.

'That's the one.' Of course, she'd seen all about it during her Aarhus research session in the car. It was a shame, in a way. He'd had no idea about the installation when he'd returned to Aarhus for the first time in twenty years, and had been blown away by the sight of it—a glass walkway, one hundred and fifty metres long, in all colours of the rainbow.

'Can we walk inside it?' Ellie asked excitedly.

'Of course,' Jesper promised.

It was as spectacular as he remembered. From inside the rainbow panorama they could see out over the city, all tinted with whichever colour they were currently standing inside. Ellie insisted on doing the walk in full rainbow order, so they started with red and made their way around.

Given her excitement about visiting the glass walkway, he'd expected her to be bubbly and full of more facts and information as they walked. But instead, she seemed to grow quieter and quieter as they made their way from red to orange to yellow to green to blue, stopping to look out at each colour change. By the time they reached indigo and violet, she'd been silent for long minutes.

Jesper stood at her side and looked out over the purple-tinted city. 'So, what do you think?'

She started at his words, as if she'd been in a world of her own. 'Um, about the rainbow? Or the message?'

'Either,' he said easily.

'I think the rainbow panorama is amazing and every city should have one,' she said. 'And as for the message… After the rain comes the rainbow? No, that's too easy. What about…

Life comes in many shades, and we need them all. Without darkness, there is no light, no colour, right?'

'That works.' He'd long since given up pretending that he had any trite messages to share about happiness from each of the places they visited, although he knew she liked to drill down to them to find the essence of each place to include in her book, or her social media captions, so that was what he tried to give her.

But for him, each of the places they went had simply given him hope at a time when he had none, and that was enough for him.

They stared out at violet Aarhus a moment longer.

Then Ellie said, 'I've been trying for more than a week to figure out how to explain the real reason I came to Denmark.'

Relief whooshed through him like a sigh and Jesper took a breath to try and figure out how to respond. 'I... I noticed. Well, I noticed that there was something you seemed to feel afraid to tell me. But I hope I'm not that scary to talk to.'

She glanced up at him over her shoulder and gave him a quick smile. 'No, not scary. And I'm not scared to tell you, exactly. More... embarrassed?'

That was something he hadn't considered—that her secret might be more of a personal humiliation than something truly terrible. He'd probably have slept better a lot of nights if he had.

'And ashamed,' Ellie went on. 'Because I know I'm being a coward about it.'

'About telling me?' Jesper asked. 'Or being in Denmark in the first place?'

'Both.' She sighed. 'The truth is…after my husband asked for a divorce, it seems he went and fell in love with my twenty-something half-sister, and now they're getting married and everyone wants me to be there to show that I give my blessing or something, but I don't think I can and so I ran away to Denmark to give myself an excuse to avoid being at their wedding.'

Jesper blinked. Whatever he'd been expecting, it really hadn't been that.

And he knew how he responded to it would shape whatever happened next between them.

Except surely there was only one way to respond to that information?

'Your ex-husband is marrying your sister?' Jesper spoke slowly, as if he was still processing the information.

'Half-sister,' Ellie corrected miserably. 'Much younger half-sister.'

He was going to pity her, she could tell. Poor, cast aside, old maid Ellie, who had not just had to watch the love of her life replace her with a younger model, but still had to see them at family gatherings.

'And your family expect you to show up at their wedding and *give your blessing?*' His voice got louder at the end, loud enough that people walking the rainbow panorama behind them stopped to look.

She really should have chosen a better place for this conversation. But something about all the colours, seeing the city in so many different ways…it had made her wonder if there was a different way to see *this*, and she'd wanted to hear Jesper's thoughts.

'Are they delusional?' Jesper asked. 'Or do they hate you for some reason?'

Ellie turned and blinked up at him, and the fury in his expression made her laugh helplessly.

'I… I don't know,' she admitted, between gasps of laughter. 'I…they just all acted like it was perfectly normal, and Mum just wants everyone to be happy, and my stepdad hates a fuss, and Maisie has always been the golden girl and they always loved Dave and they were so angry when we got divorced—with me, even though he was the one who left. I think Mum thought I should have done more to keep him happy, that I'd concentrated on my career instead of my marriage, or that it was because we'd never had kids, and… I don't know. It just all felt like my fault, and now I'm avoiding Mum's calls because she just makes me feel awful and guilty for not wanting to be there.'

The words had just tumbled out of her in a rush, like a waterfall, and all that was left behind when they were done was an overwhelming sense of relief. It was all out there now, for him to think what he wanted about it.

But she'd been honest about how she felt for the first time. And that felt amazing.

'Guilty,' Jesper repeated incredulously. Well, she'd told him she was a people pleaser. Now he got to see how far that ridiculous trait had taken her.

'Even when Lily asked, I told her I was fine with it all,' she said, trying not to laugh at herself. How ridiculous she'd been, and not even realised. Of course she wasn't fine with it. Who would be? 'I don't think she believed me, but, well. Dave and I were already over when he and Maisie got together, so...what could I do?'

'Are you sure about that?' Jesper asked sharply. 'That they only got together after your divorce, I mean?'

'They said so,' Ellie replied. 'They were adamant about it. And honestly? If they were together when we were still married... I'm not sure I want to know.'

She would have, back then, though. Back when she still loved him. And it would have broken her.

Now? Now the idea just left her with a vaguely sick feeling in her stomach.

'You're ready to move on,' Jesper said softly. 'That's why you don't want to know.'

She stopped, and considered. 'I guess... I am. You're right.'

That was good news, right? She'd kind of thought she *had* moved on—physically, at least. She'd left her job, gone freelance, moved to Denmark for four months... Moving had been taking place. But she realised that, inside, she was still back where she had been the day Dave had told her he was leaving, and still reliving the day when her mum had told her about Maisie marrying him.

It was nice to think that, finally, she might be

able to move past all that to whatever happened next. Like this rainbow marked the end of that storm, and the promise of something better to follow. Wasn't that what rainbows meant? That God would never send another flood, or something. Or, in this context, that the universe would never let her half-sister marry her ex-husband again. Which, she had to admit, was pretty niche.

Maybe just that if she moved past this storm it was all sunshine and rainbows from here on in.

She'd take that.

Ellie smiled up at Jesper, but his expression was still serious, as though he had something more to say, so she waited to hear what it was. She'd not regretted listening to him yet, and she didn't imagine she was about to start now.

'I understand a little better now, I think, about you not wanting to make your happiness contingent on another person,' he said slowly. 'It was different for me. But here…it's like your ex-husband took your happy life and gave it to another person. Your sister.'

'I… I hadn't thought about it that way,' Ellie admitted. 'But yes, I guess so.'

'But has it occurred to you…in your determination to not attach your happiness to another person, you're attaching your *unhappiness* to one? Well, two really.'

She stared up at him, his words sinking slowly through the protective layers of hardened emotions she'd surrounded herself with since the divorce.

She'd been so focused on finding happiness, she hadn't even considered the act of discarding unhappiness. She'd buried it deep instead, and tried to cover it over with rainbows and trolls and sunsets and the like. But Jesper was right. It was dragging her down, keeping her from ever finding true happiness, because she couldn't move past that moment when she'd realised that she wasn't enough.

That Dave had chosen younger, prettier, perkier Maisie over her, and cast Ellie on the scrapheap.

'She's pregnant, you know.' She blurted the words out, that last bit of pain stabbing her. 'He and I, we never did. We didn't want kids, we knew that from the start. But she... I'm not supposed to know, but my other sister let it slip. Maisie is pregnant and that's why they're getting married so fast.'

Ellie had never wavered in her decision not to have children. It wasn't the right path for her.

But now...was her mother right? Was Maisie giving him everything she couldn't?

Had she failed?

And, if so, how could she ever hope to succeed at anything again?

Jesper reached out and grabbed her forearms, pulling her square with him so she had no real choice but to look up into his eyes. The way they held each other's arms felt like some sort of Viking promise or oath, and normally she'd have laughed at the very idea, but now didn't feel like a time for laughing.

It felt like a time for revelation.

'Your life, your future, your happiness, it's not about them any more,' he said, his voice soft but firm. 'Let them live their lives—you don't owe them anything more than that, no blessings, whatever anyone says. But let them get on and do whatever they want. Because *your* life, your future, your happiness... Ellie, it's going to be so much better than anything you had before.'

His words seemed to settle over her before being absorbed by her mind, her body, the truth of them sinking into every inch of her.

She *was* going to have a happier, better life than before. Because she wasn't twenty-two any longer, like she'd been when she'd said yes to Dave's proposal, shackling her whole life to his. She wasn't a twenty-something newbie journalist desperate to learn the ropes and live the city life. She wasn't the submissive daughter who had to do whatever it took to keep the peace, the same way her mum always had. She wasn't the woman who worked so hard not to let anyone down, even if it meant letting *herself* down.

She wasn't any of the women she'd been before in her life.

She was Ellie. A forty-four-year-old divorcee, living her own life on her own terms for the first time in decades, maybe ever. She was carving a new career writing about things that mattered to her, influencing other women finding themselves after years lost in marriage or motherhood or careers that didn't appreciate them or parents or spouses or friends who tried to control them…

She was Ellie. And she was going to be happy.

However she saw fit.

'I really want to kiss you right now,' she whispered.

Jesper smiled. 'I've been waiting for you to say that for days.'

Then he dipped his head, pausing at the last

moment to give her a chance to pull away, in case this wasn't really what she wanted.

But she didn't.

And kissing a gorgeous man under a glass rainbow felt more spectacular than anything the old Ellie had ever experienced.

CHAPTER EIGHT

JESPER HAD REMEMBERED that kissing Ellie felt wonderful. But this…this was something else.

He knew her now. Understood her, perhaps. Felt a part of her life.

When he'd kissed her on New Year's Eve, it had been sweet and nice and had woken up parts of him long dormant. But he could still have walked away without harm.

This time when their lips met, he knew that one kiss was never going to be enough.

He'd told himself, over and over, that he was only doing this, this quest, for Ellie. To help her. But now, kissing her, he had to admit it had been for him, too. To make the last few years of his introspection and isolation mean something for someone other than him.

And to be near her, just a little while longer. To have the chance to maybe, maybe hold her again like this.

Finally, though, he had to pull away. 'We should…we need to get out of here.'

Ellie looked around, her eyes dazed, then nodded. 'Back to the apartment. Now.'

Heat surged through him as he realised what she was suggesting. 'Are you sure?'

She met his gaze with her own direct one. 'Very.'

They made it back to the apartment in record time. Jesper didn't think he'd let go of Ellie's hand the whole way.

'There are all sorts of things we're missing seeing at the art gallery, you know,' he said as they hurried across the street.

She gave him an incredulous look. 'Do you really care about that right now?'

'Hell, no.'

And he didn't. This, her, in his arms, wanting him the way he wanted her, it was all he'd been dreaming about for days.

But that didn't seem to stop his head from interrupting the bliss his body was chasing.

She doesn't want anything serious. That's good. Neither do I. She hasn't been with anyone since her husband, I'm guessing. And I haven't been with anyone since Agnes. But that was a lot longer ago than her divorce… What if

she has been with people since then? I mean...
Good for her, I guess. But it means I'm really
out of practice.

He shook away the running commentary in
his head. It wasn't as if making love was something he could forget how to do. And besides,
he'd been imagining all the ways he'd kiss and
touch her—and hating himself for it—every
night after she went to bed. He knew what to
do.

As long as she was sure this was what she
wanted.

The apartment door slammed shut behind
them and her lips were on his in an instant,
the pair of them walking—her backwards, him
forwards—towards his room as they kissed.
After the last couple of weeks of not kissing,
it seemed impossible to stop now, even for a
moment.

But he had to.

He tore his lips away as the back of her knees
hit his bed, and refused to be swayed by her
needy, desperate look.

'Are you sure you want to do this?' He tried
to sound serious but, given the way he was
panting, he wasn't sure he pulled it off.

'Are you kidding me?' She reached up and

grabbed the back of his neck, trying to pull him down for another kiss.

But Jesper held firm. 'I need to hear the words. Because you told me…you were adamant that we couldn't do this, that it would ruin your whole quest, your project. And if you want it now because we talked about your ex and you need to feel desired or something…trust me, I desire you. I want you so badly it hurts. But if it isn't what *you* want, then we need to stop now. Because the worst thing for me would be you regretting it afterwards.'

Ellie's grip on the back of his neck softened, and she dropped down from her tiptoes so she was even shorter than him than she had been before. But she kept her gaze fixed on his, searching his face for something.

'You really mean that, don't you?' she whispered, and he realised she was going to take the out. She was going to put the brakes on and think about this some more.

And however much it felt like parts of him might actually fall off from frustration, if that was what she wanted then it was the right thing.

'I really do,' he promised.

She swallowed, and glanced down for just a moment, before looking up and meeting his eyes again with a fiery certainty.

'Then trust me when I tell you, I've never wanted anything as much as I want you inside me right now.'

That was all the reassurance Jesper needed.

Ellie hadn't given much thought to what it might be like to have sex with a Viking. She had, however, given considerable thought to the question of what it would be like to have sex with Jesper. Now she'd experienced the latter, she knew that they were in no way the same thing.

A Viking pillaged and plundered, right? Took what they wanted and then left.

Jesper, on the other hand, gave far, far more than he took. Even if she did feel rather plundered the morning after.

Also, he hadn't gone anywhere.

Ellie stretched carefully against his sheets, checking in with her body for every sign of the night—and afternoon, if she was honest— they'd spent together. The ache in her thigh muscles, and the beard burn on the skin over them. The reddened skin of her breasts where he'd lavished her nipples with attention with his tongue until her toes curled. The deep-seated contentment in her chest, and the heavy, relaxed feeling in her whole body from just too many orgasms.

All right, not *too* many. Just a lot more than she'd had in one go in a really long time.

She'd been nervous at first—well, at first, she'd just been desperate to kiss him, to feel him, to *have* him. But after his last attempt at chivalry, when he'd suggested they hold back if she wasn't sure…after she'd convinced him she was *very* sure, all bets had been off. It had been a while since she'd had any man's focused attention on her, and Jesper had certainly been very focused.

It was hardly surprising he was still passed out cold on the bed next to her. The man had put in a shift and a half since they'd landed on his bed the afternoon before.

She twisted on her side to watch him sleeping, the silver in his hair and beard glinting in the morning light, but the crow's feet around his eyes smoothed out by sleep so that he looked younger than she'd seen him before. It amazed her that this man, who'd suffered such loss, could still talk so freely of happiness. Could show her the path to her own joy.

'Your life, your future, your happiness, it's not about them any more,' he'd said. *'Let them get on and do whatever they want. Because*

your life, your future, your happiness... Ellie, it's going to be so much better than anything you had before.'

Was he right? She hoped so. And in that moment when he'd said it...she'd believed it with her whole heart.

That was why she'd given in and kissed him. Not because he spoke a lot of pretty words, but because he made her believe them—made her believe in herself.

Something she was going to have to learn to do on her own, she knew. But just for now...it was nice to have the help.

And this morning? She felt more powerful, more desired, more in control of her own destiny than she had in for ever.

This wasn't about making her happiness contingent on another person. And it certainly wasn't about doing whatever someone else wanted to keep the peace, or keep their love. This was something else.

She wasn't quite sure what to call it yet, but she knew it felt real.

Beside her, Jesper stirred, his bright blue eyes blinking open. He smiled when he saw her still naked beside him. Ellie considered pulling the sheets up to cover her more, but didn't.

God bless Danish housing and its overactive heating systems.

'Good morning,' he said, his voice raspy. 'Sleep well?'

'Wonderfully,' she assured him.

She only noticed the tension in his shoulders as it disappeared at her words.

'You thought I was going to regret this?' she asked.

'I really hoped not,' he joked. 'Because if you did, we wouldn't get to do it again, and that would be a crying shame.'

'It would,' she agreed as his arm snaked out to wrap around her middle and pull her body flush against his again. 'You know, I thought I'd feel self-conscious, being naked with a strange man for the first time since my divorce, but I don't.'

'I object to the term *strange* in that sentence,' Jesper replied. 'But I'm glad you don't feel self-conscious. It would also be a travesty for you to cover up that wonderful body again.'

Ellie felt a flush of pink to her cheeks that might have been to do with his words, or the Danish heating system, or maybe the way he was pressing his hardness against her stomach, showing her how much he wanted her again.

And probably again, if last night was anything to go by.

She knew that men's recovery time lengthened the older they got, but it seemed to her that Jesper had some brilliant ideas on how to pass the time in between...

Her body wasn't the same as it had been at twenty-two, she knew that. She'd lived half her life since then, and long since waved farewell to the perfectly smooth skin, vibrant chestnut hair and flat stomach she'd had back then. Maybe she could have retained it all with a celebrity's skincare, diet and exercise routine, not to mention their hairdresser on call, but Ellie had always felt that there were more important things in life than how she looked.

Besides, she *liked* that her face and body showed that she'd lived. Experienced. Grown and thought and learned and *been*. She looked like who she was.

And while she might have doubted her value as a forty-something woman post-divorce for a little while, one night with Jesper had definitely reminded her of everything she loved about her body.

'What are you thinking?' he asked in a ticklish whisper by her ear, before he lowered his lips to kiss her neck. 'You have the most *devilish* smile on your face.'

'Just how glad I am we are here,' she replied. 'I think… I needed this. I didn't realise it—tried to resist it, even. But I needed something to remind me of who I am, and what this body is capable of.'

'Glad to be of service.' He placed one last kiss on her collarbone then pulled back, sitting up against the headboard. 'Does this mean sex with me is just a part of your happiness quest? Is last night going in your book?'

She laughed. 'Definitely not.' Experiencing great sex was one thing. Writing about it for thousands of people to read was another. 'I'm sure I can find some discreet euphemisms to use.'

'You're the writer.' He wasn't meeting her eye any more, and Ellie realised she'd said something wrong.

Sitting up beside him, one leg folded under her as she looked at him, she ran back through the conversation to figure out what it was.

'I didn't sleep with you because it was a step on my happiness quest,' she said bluntly.

He raised an eyebrow. 'Are you sure? It's the only reason you're here with me. It would make sense. And I'm not exactly complaining.'

Maybe not, but she could tell he didn't like it all the same.

Ellie reached over and grabbed his hand, toying with his fingers. 'This, us…this was just for me. Not for the blog or the book. Or for revenge against Dave and Maisie. Or any other reason except that I really, really wanted it. Wanted you.'

His fingers tightened around hers. 'I'm glad.'

'You were right, yesterday,' she went on. 'My happiness is up to me now. And whatever I choose to do with it isn't contingent on another person any more. And right now I'm choosing this. Us. You.'

He gave her a small one-sided smile. 'I'm sensing a *but* there.'

She hadn't known she had a caveat to that until he'd pointed it out. The moment she considered it, there it was, waiting for her to realise.

'But I'm leaving next month.'

'As soon as the wedding is over, right?'

She nodded. 'Not because…not because this is just about running away any more. But because I've been hiding out long enough, and it's time to find my real future.'

'Somewhere else.' There was a strange, sad look on his face, one she couldn't quite read.

But she understood it, all the same. It was the knowledge that anything between them was over before it had really even started. Because she couldn't just throw herself into another relationship. She needed to finish finding who she was, the new woman in her new life, first.

She shifted closer to him, folding herself in against his side so his arm came around her and she could feel his heartbeat under the hand she placed on his chest.

'Remember at the rainbow yesterday, we talked about the contrasts of happiness? Light after dark. The sunshine after the rain.'

'I remember.' His chest reverberated with his words. She got the feeling that Jesper would remember every moment of that trip for a long time.

She knew she would. It had changed her whole view of the world.

'I realised that I can remember the happy times I had with Dave, the person I was then and how I grew, without the memories being ruined by how it ended.' That sounded very fully visualised and grown woman, didn't it? 'Well, I hope I will be able to, one day soon, anyway,' she added, needing to be honest with herself as well as him.

'That's good,' Jesper said. 'That's a really good thing. I want that for you.'

Did he have it for himself? Was he able to think about his wife without remembering the sickening moment when he knew she was dead? Or regretting so many things that came before? Ellie didn't know.

She hoped so. But given the few things he'd said about the state of his marriage before her death, she wasn't sure.

And if he couldn't...maybe she could help him find a way to being able to.

'I want to enjoy this while we can have it.' She pressed herself firmly against his side so he knew exactly what she was talking about. 'Like the fairytale romance while it lasts.'

'And when it's over?' he asked.

'Then I might miss it—I *will* miss it. But I can look back on it fondly, too.' She smiled up at him a little sadly. 'Maybe making a bank of happy memories is a part of finding happiness. Good, happy thoughts to get you through the harder times.'

'Maybe it is,' he agreed.

Ellie bit her lip before asking, 'Is that how you feel about your wife now?' Because if he had managed it, surely she could too.

But Jesper's muscles stiffened underneath

her touch, the room suddenly cooler and darker, even though the winter sky outside hadn't changed.

'I'm sure I will,' he said shortly. He pulled away, swinging his legs out of the bed. 'Come on. We should pack.'

Ellie blinked up at him, thrown by the sudden change of topic and tone. 'I thought we were staying in Aarhus a few days?'

'We were.' Jesper already had a towel around his waist and was heading for the en suite bathroom. 'But you mentioned a fairytale. I know what I want to show you next. And I happen to know a fantastic hotel in Odense.'

And then he was gone, into the bathroom, leaving Ellie still naked on the bed, confused and concerned about what had just happened.

Odense sat on the central Danish island of Fyn, between the mainland and Zealand, where Copenhagen was. It was another city Jesper knew relatively well, and it didn't have the same connotations with Agnes and her family that Aarhus did.

And right then, he really needed to not think about his dead wife.

Besides, the First Grand Hotel really was a fantastic place to stay, and he couldn't let Ellie leave Denmark without experiencing Hans Christian Andersen's home village, nearby.

That was what this was about. Ellie's quest, and her book—everything she needed to discover and achieve here in Denmark before it was time for her to leave. And as they drove back across the bridge to Fyn, Jesper clasped his hands tight on the wheel and reminded himself of that again and again.

Because he'd got too close to forgetting, lying in bed with her that morning.

He'd known, going into this, what Ellie could offer him. And he'd known how much he could take, too. But for a moment there he'd been truly happy, wrapped up around her naked body.

Until she'd asked about Agnes.

It wasn't guilt that had filled him, or grief. He'd made his peace with her death as well as he could reasonably expect to.

No, it was the realisation that Ellie had already reached the point where she could think back fondly on her marriage—maybe not all the time, he wasn't imagining that one night with him had performed that kind of miracle— but he hadn't.

Three years of solitude and inner work and still, when he thought of Agnes, he remembered all the ways that he had failed, and everything he should have done differently.

Maybe Ellie didn't feel that way because she hadn't done anything wrong. It seemed to him that her ex-husband was the failure in that marriage, not that he imagined *he* was feeling the kind of guilt that Jesper himself carried.

But he'd realised in that moment that even if he couldn't move past the wrongs he'd committed in his past, Ellie was on the right path. And it was his job to keep her walking it.

He couldn't pull her down with him.

Their next destination on the happiness quest had suddenly been clear in his head, and he'd started moving, keen to keep her on track. Why waste what little time they had together? And as much as he liked Aarhus…it held a lot of memories for him, and he'd wanted a little distance between him and them, too.

It was only later, when he saw the puzzled frown line between her brows, that he'd realised she might have taken his sudden burst of movement the wrong way. But it was too late to do much about that now.

Better to keep moving.

'Are you…is everything okay?' Ellie's voice was tentative and she sat in his passenger seat looking uncertain if she was even supposed to be there.

Damn. He'd screwed this up. Already.

It might be a new record.

'It's fine.' A lie, and they both knew it.

'Only you're gripping that steering wheel rather tight. Your knuckles are white.' She gave a tiny laugh, as if it might a joke, but the humour evaporated in the thick air of tension in the car.

Jesper sucked in a breath, trying to remember some of the mindful breathing exercises he'd done on a breathwork retreat a couple of years before.

This wasn't fair to Ellie. He wasn't being fair.

She'd told him her truth. He owed her more of his, too.

She'd be gone soon. And he was wasting this time with her.

He sighed, and tried to hold the steering wheel a little more loosely. 'I'm sorry. I just… when you asked about Agnes, I realised you've made more progress moving on from your marriage over the past couple of weeks than I have in the last three years.'

He sneaked a glance over at her and saw her blink three times in rapid succession.

'I'm not sure that's true,' she said slowly. 'But

even if it were…my circumstances are rather different.'

'I know.' He sighed again. 'I'm being ridiculous. I just… There are things I haven't told you about my marriage.'

'Would you like to?' she asked carefully. 'Tell me, I mean?'

Jesper swallowed. 'I think I might.'

It was easier to talk while driving, somehow. Maybe because he didn't have to look at Ellie as he spoke, and only caught glimpses of her reactions out of the corner of his eye.

'Agnes and I, we met in Aarhus, where her family lived at the time. I told you that, yes?' He checked to see if she remembered, and continued when she nodded. 'Her family had money, far more money than anyone I'd ever met before, and it was as if she lived in a different world. But she wasn't spoilt or entitled particularly— her family liked to use their wealth to help people. And it made me want to do the same. I wanted to be rich and successful so that I could help people too.'

'That's…admirable?' Ellie sounded as if she wasn't sure, as if she was waiting for the other shoe to drop.

She wouldn't have to wait long.

'I was offered a job over in America, and

we moved there together. To start with, it was wonderful. Agnes made new friends, went new places. We both got used to living the high life. I branched out and started my own firm, and had even more success than I'd had before—and more money too. We used it for philanthropic projects, as well as our own comfort and fun, just as I'd always planned. We were living the life we'd dreamed of.'

He paused for a moment, the memories stinging inside his chest, his eyes raw with remembering.

Ellie didn't interrupt, didn't try to guess the ending, even though she knew exactly where it was heading. Maybe she guessed that there was another twist to come before the tragic conclusion.

'I became… Agnes said obsessed. I wanted to do better. Make more, give more. I was working all the hours God sent, leaving her to represent us at galas and charity events. I made the money, she gave it away. I thought it was the right thing to do, but…she resented the time it took. I was too busy earning the money to hang off her arm at the galas and charity balls. I wasn't interested in that part and, honestly, I didn't have the time.' Now he knew why his eyes hurt. It wasn't the memories. It was the tears he'd been holding back for so long.

He couldn't let them fall now. He had to get through this.

Still, in the interest of safety, he pulled over at the next opportunity. Even if it meant having to look at Ellie while he spoke.

'Sounds like she wanted to have her cake and eat it.' She said it mildly, as if she was afraid to speak ill of the dead. 'She wanted you to earn a lot of money but resented the time it took. She didn't like the trade-off.'

Jesper shook his head. 'I just wasn't good enough. I couldn't give her what she needed.'

'I don't think anybody could.' Ellie's hand rested on his thigh, rubbing small circles on his leg.

'Maybe.' He wasn't sure he could believe it, though. 'I always knew I had something of an addictive personality. My parents...neither of them ever did anything by half measures. My father used to say you had to be all-in or all-out, nothing in between was worth anything. You might not be surprised to learn that he was not your typical Dane.'

'No, I can see that. As a nation, you've got more of a reputation for balance.'

Balance. Exactly what he'd been looking

for the past few years—and thought that he'd found, until Ellie came along.

'I lost any sense of it when we were over in the States. All I could think about was work, but I was so *happy* there, living that life. And Agnes…she grew to hate it.' He took a breath. 'She tried to talk to me, I think. But I couldn't listen. No, I *wouldn't* listen. So she left me. She was on her way to the airport by the time I came home and found the note. But she never got there because…there was a car crash. She was killed instantly.'

'Jesper, I'm so sorry.' Her hand tightened on his leg.

'That's not the end of the story.' This was the hardest part—the part he'd never told anybody. That only he and one doctor at the New York hospital where Agnes had been treated knew. God, he was glad he wasn't driving right now. 'She was pregnant when she died. She…it wasn't something we'd been trying for, and she didn't tell me before she went. I don't even know for sure that she knew herself. But I think she did. I think that was why she was leaving. Because she knew that I couldn't be what a child needed. I couldn't be what anyone needed.'

'You were what I needed.' Ellie's voice was

SOPHIE PEMBROKE   **189**

small, quiet, and he almost missed her words. 'When you agreed to take me on this happiness quest…you were exactly what I needed.'

He gave her a small, sad smile. 'For now.'

It wouldn't last—couldn't last. She would leave as planned soon enough and he'd be alone again.

And that, Jesper realised, was only for the best.

'I'm so sorry.' She sounded almost as broken as he felt.

With an incredible force of will, Jesper pushed it all aside. He didn't want Agnes to hang like a spectre over what little time he had left with Ellie.

'It just threw me off-balance,' he said. 'I'll be fine when we get to Odense.' He'd never visited Odense with Agnes, he wasn't sure why. But there were no memories lurking there for him.

'If you want to get separate rooms at the hotel there—I mean, maybe you were planning that anyway, I don't want to presume,' Ellie said. 'But if you want me to stay away, I'll understand. Last night…it doesn't have to mean anything.'

But it did. It meant an awful lot and Jesper wasn't willing to give that up, even if maybe he should.

'I don't want that.' He tried to give her a smile but from her pained expression, he wasn't very successful. 'Agnes…she's been gone a long time. I know I need to move on, and I have in lots of ways. It just still surprises me sometimes.'

'I can understand that,' Ellie said softly.

'But that doesn't mean I don't value being here with you, right now,' he went on. 'Because I do, very much. This…this adventure with you has made me feel more like myself than I have in years. And the connection between us—I know it can't last, but I don't want to give it up a moment before we have to.'

Ellie blew out a breath he guessed was relief. 'That's…that's good. Because neither do I, really. Being with you—I mean our travels as well as last night—it's been helping me find my way back to myself, too. But I think I have a little further to go still, you know? And I hope we can still help each other get there, until I have to go home to London.'

'Then that's what we'll do,' Jesper promised. 'Together.'

He felt lighter for telling her the truth. He wondered if this was how she had felt after confessing about her ex in the rainbow panorama the day before. If so, he could understand better what had happened next.

It was exhilarating, opening up to another person—and being understood. He felt closer to Ellie than he had to anyone in such a long time. This shared journey had connected them in ways he'd never expected.

He just needed to remember what would happen when she left. Once this was over, he still needed to be able to keep himself on an even keel. He knew now that the temptation to throw himself into work, or another project, would be overwhelming.

Maybe that was what his first attempt at going off-grid, seeking happiness, had been too, at its heart. Something to replace the work he'd left behind.

But now he knew better. Life wasn't all extremes—it couldn't be. He needed to find balance.

Perhaps he needed this happiness quest as much as Ellie did.

Either way, they were in this together. And he wasn't going to lose that before he had to.

He just needed to hold on and not let himself fall in too deep.

How hard could that be?

CHAPTER NINE

THE FIRST GRAND HOTEL, right in the centre of Odense, was very grand indeed—from its red brick facade to the elegant luxury of its reception lobby, the smooth and reassuring presence of the staff and the gold trimmed lift that took them up to the best suite the hotel had to offer, the moment Jesper handed over his credit card.

Ellie hadn't really stopped to think all that much about exactly how rich Jesper was, but she supposed that a person couldn't afford to go off-grid and not work for two or three years unless they were sitting on a significant nest egg.

Still, she didn't think today was the day to ask about it.

After his confession in the car, at least some of the tension that had been pulled taut between them since they'd left the apartment in Aarhus had dissipated. She felt she understood him better now. And despite the fact they'd spent so much of the journey discussing his late wife, the same way they'd talked about her ex-husband the day before, somehow, talking it through seemed to diminish Agnes' shadow rather than deepen it.

She hoped that Jesper felt the same. That by putting it all out in the open between them it had brought them closer together, rather than pushing them apart.

All the same, when he'd asked for the suite— a suite which came with two bedrooms, she noted—Ellie had fully expected him to retreat into one of them for some time alone before they began whatever his next outing was. The Hans Christian Andersen Museum, she thought he'd said, although at the time she'd been too busy obsessing over what she'd done wrong to really listen.

But she *hadn't* done anything wrong. And neither had he, really. It was just that they both had their past lives hanging over them whether they liked it or not, and that wasn't ever going to change. A consequence of living, she supposed. When you had that flush of first love in your teens and twenties, you only had all the ways your parents or childhood had screwed you up to contend with. By the time you were in your forties, you had to add another twenty years of your own mess-ups and other people's idiocy to the mix. It wasn't a thing you could simply overlook.

So Ellie was prepared for a quiet evening working on the book, maybe taking a bubble bath and ordering some room service, if Jesper deigned to come out and join her. But, to her surprise, the moment the bellboy had left their baggage and shut the door to the suite behind him, Jesper darted across the room and wrapped his arms around her middle from behind, his lips already on her neck.

Her blood grew warmer with every kiss. 'Are you sure you—' He pressed himself more firmly against her backside. 'Oh. Very sure, then.'

And if he wanted this, who was she to argue? Especially since she wanted it just as much.

Needed it too, she thought as she turned in his arms to kiss his lips. Needed the connection between them that had been strained by his unexpected behaviour that morning. A physical connection to match the emotional one they'd forged through their conversations.

Maybe Jesper knew that was what she needed, too. Because after he led her to the largest of the two bedrooms the suite had to offer, he laid her out over the silken, embroidered bedspread and took the time to remind every single inch of her how much he wanted her. As if he was memorising her, she realised. So he couldn't forget.

She surged up underneath him, wrapping an arm around his neck as she kissed him, deeply. 'My turn,' she murmured, and promptly manoeuvred him onto his back—not an easy feat given the height and weight advantage he had over her. But luckily, he didn't seem to object enough to try and stop her.

Certainly, he seemed to have no problem at all with the way she kissed a trail down his chest, her hands running over his skin as she went, memorising him the way he had her.

After all, if they only had this time together, hadn't she vowed to make the most of every second?

Later—quite a lot later, if Ellie was honest—she realised they still hadn't eaten.

'Did you want to get some dinner?' She propped herself up on one elbow to look at him as she asked the question. His eyes were closed, but she was pretty sure he wasn't asleep. He was breathing quite heavily, though, which was fair enough.

It had been a very energetic afternoon.

'Did you want to go out?' he asked, without

opening his eyes. 'I know some great restaurants in Odense.'

That sounded nice; she loved sitting across from him in restaurants, getting to know each other a little more with every mouthful. And she wasn't above enjoying the way that other women—and more than a few men—looked at them together with a shade of envy.

But going out involved getting showered. And dressed. And probably putting on make-up and nice shoes for the sort of restaurants Jesper likely knew in the city.

And the bed really was very comfortable…

'We could get room service?' she suggested.

Jesper groaned in what she quickly realised was relief. 'Oh, thank God, yes, please. I don't think I can leave this room for at least a day. Maybe more. You've broken me, woman.'

She snickered, and placed a kiss against his temple as she went to find the room service menu. 'Oh, dear,' she said with false sympathy. 'I guess we'd better not do that again, then.'

He sat up with alarming alacrity. 'Now, hang on, I didn't say that…' He reached for her, and Ellie dodged out of the way, giggling as she held the room service menu out of reach.

And she realised, as he caught her around the

waist and pulled her back down to the bed and into his arms, that she was happy. Truly happy.

Was that what exorcising ghosts and secrets could give them? Happiness?

Maybe. Either way, just for this moment, she could let herself be happy. It wasn't a quest or a challenge or a puzzle to solve, it just *was*.

She knew it couldn't last. Even if she wasn't going back to London soon, happiness with another person never did. They'd become entrenched and bored and have all the problems couples faced. She could only be this happy right now because she knew it was fleeting.

But maybe she could hold onto it a little bit longer.

'You know, I think I like Odense,' she said, snuggling back into her pillow.

Jesper brushed her hair away from her face with a smile. 'You haven't seen anything of it yet.'

'I don't need to,' she replied. 'I'm happy, just here.'

For a moment his eyes widened, and then darkened as his pupils grew. 'Me too.'

'Maybe…maybe we could stay here, just for a little while,' she suggested. 'Before we head back to Copenhagen.'

The wedding was in two weeks, and she'd

booked her return ticket for nine days after, in the hope it made it less obvious she was only there to avoid the wedding. She'd have no reason to stay beyond that, and she knew that once they were back in the city she'd be counting down the days until she left.

But here? Time sort of disappeared. And she liked that.

'I think we can manage that,' Jesper said, and leaned in to kiss her again. 'I'm sure we'll manage to fill the time somehow…'

It was rather a lot later *again* before they got around to ordering room service.

It took them a while to make it to the Hans Christian Andersen Museum that Jesper had promised Ellie they'd visit. In fairness, he didn't think it was entirely his fault. Neither of them had wanted to stray too far from the hotel room—or from each other—for a while. The café down the road and the hotel restaurant was about as far as they'd made it from the bed for the best part of a week.

Ellie's social media posts had relied heavily on photos taken from the rainbow panorama, the morning or evening light from their hotel window, and arty shots of coffees and pastries for the last few days. The captions though, to

Jesper's mind, had seemed more authentically her than any he'd read before. Even if she hadn't mentioned him at all—which he understood. Ellie's journey here was about *her*, not him.

But last night, as they'd lain in each other's arms in the darkness, Ellie had said, 'I think it's time to go back to Copenhagen, isn't it?'

He'd wanted to say no, wanted to keep them in this private bubble of bliss for just a little longer. But he knew she was right. Her stay in Denmark was finite after all, and it wasn't all about him. She'd want to spend time with Lily. She would need to pack up her apartment before she left. And it wasn't as if she'd spent a lot of the last week writing either.

Of course she needed to get back to reality. And he probably should too, as much as he hated the idea.

'We'll leave tomorrow,' he'd said with a heavy heart. 'We can stop at the Hans Christian Andersen Museum on our way.'

He'd felt her smile against his skin, where her cheek rested on his chest. 'You're determined we're going to get there, aren't you?'

'I think you have to indulge in the fairytale before we leave, don't you?'

'I think I already have,' she'd replied.

And now they were here.

The place was more of an art installation than a museum, an immersive experience that pulled them into the fairytale world Andersen had created, using light and sound and texture and possibly magic, Jesper wasn't sure. Ellie certainly looked captivated, enthralled even, and he couldn't help but think about the day in the rainbow panorama, and how it had changed their entire relationship.

He couldn't shake the feeling that this experience might, too. And not in such a good way.

If the rainbow walkway over Aarhus had given Ellie the courage to open up to him, and to risk kissing him again, he could feel the fairytale experience drawing her away from him. She was already picturing her next life—he could see the hope and the excitement in her expression.

She was getting ready to move on. To write her own fairytale. To take the world and the happiness he'd shown her, and apply it to her real life back in London.

Without him.

He should be happy for her. He *was* happy for her—he wanted her to live the life that brought her joy. He was glad he'd been able to help her move on from her ex-husband, to see that her family's expectations of her blessing his remarriage were unreasonable and that she didn't have to give in to them. He was especially glad that he'd been the one to help her appreciate that physical pleasure and connection with another didn't mean you were putting all of your faith and happiness in that one person. That you could stay your own self, even when you were with others—and you didn't have to sacrifice what you wanted to make that other person stay.

Except that last was exactly why he *couldn't* ask her to stay longer. Ellie was ready to go home—or she would be, when the time came—and he couldn't, wouldn't stop her.

Not least because he knew he had nothing to offer beyond what they'd enjoyed these last few weeks.

He couldn't fall in love with her, couldn't give over his life to her the way he had to his work before. He knew that he wasn't capable of being what someone else needed—he'd tried with Agnes, and look how that had ended up. He couldn't promise her anything more than a casual, friendly arrangement with great sex. And Ellie wanted the fairytale—he could see it in her face now. She might have been adamant that she wouldn't hang her happiness on another person, but he knew that once she had that happiness as a bedrock of her soul she'd want to share it.

She would find someone who could love her the way she deserved to be loved. Someone who wasn't him.

And he was happy he'd helped her get to the point where she was ready for that.

Really, he was.

Even if part of him wanted to beg her to stay longer. Not for ever, just…longer.

He swallowed back the impulse when she bounded towards him, beaming. He wasn't going to ruin this moment for her, or bring down their last days together.

'Isn't this place amazing?' Ellie grabbed his hand and swung back around, still trying to drink in every inch of the place. 'I'm so glad you brought me here.'

'I'm glad too.' His voice was raspy; he'd been thinking too long, not talking with her. He should have been experiencing this with her instead of standing back and watching.

'We can visit Hans Christian Andersen's childhood home too, while we're here. If you want?' Ellie looked up at him with wide eyes, and he couldn't say anything but yes, of course.

But he regretted it when he saw the humble home where Andersen had grown up. The poverty and hardship he'd been raised in. The terrible, tragic life that had perhaps inspired some aspects of his tales, like the bed where his father had died, while Andersen lay shivering on the floor, believing the ice maiden had taken him.

Jesper had never lived that life. But he had made his own fortune; his parents had no money to spare, especially after his father had finished spending it, gambling or drinking or just 'treating' them. Money had flowed out of his hands faster than it came in, because his father had always felt that life was for living and money was for spending.

Jesper had never had to look too far to see where his tendency for extremes came from. Remembering his childhood with his parents was like looking in a mirror. For them, it had been life and fun. For him, it had turned out to be work. But it was all the same in the end.

Agnes has been born into money, had always had it so never wanted for or worried about it.

Had that been the difference between them? He couldn't help dwelling on the idea as Ellie moved around the small cottage, learning about Andersen's life.

He'd always known that money mattered, that he had to sacrifice to get it, that he needed to make it to keep her, to keep them in the way she'd expected and he'd come to appreciate. She hadn't been materialistic or grasping or anything like that. But she'd always had enough and wouldn't understand *not* having it. She'd have gone to her family to ask for more, and Jesper...he could never have done that.

So he'd worked for it instead. He'd worked and worked and thrown himself into the business and been a success and he'd never known when to stop. Never realised that she was waiting for him to finish, to come home to her.

That was when the problems had started. It wasn't money, he knew that really. It was his obsessions, his tendency to go to extremes. That was what had ruined his life, had killed Agnes in the end.

He couldn't risk that again.

Ellie was still absorbed in the museum so Jesper leaned on the nearest doorframe and watched her, struck by the difference between the fairytale experience and this house. It felt like the contrast between his time with Ellie— the fairytale—and what would come next, the moment she was gone.

He'd be alone again. He needed to...he needed to figure out how he was going to do that.

Because he'd done what he always did— what he'd sworn he'd never do again.

He'd gone too far, too fast. Taken things to

extremes. Gone off the deep end to the exclusion of everything else.

He'd made his whole world about Ellie and her quest.

He'd fallen in love with her.

And now he had to make damn sure he fell out of love before she left, or it was going to break him.

Love was too risky an emotion for the likes of him.

'Are you ready?' He blinked, and realised that Ellie was right in front of him, speaking to him, and looking up at him with concern in her eyes.

'Ready?' he asked, knowing he sounded confused.

'To go, I mean. Back to Copenhagen. I think I'm done here if you are,' she said. 'Or we can grab a coffee from the café before we leave?'

'No. No, let's get on the road. We can stop for coffee on the way.' The car was all packed up, and it was time to head back to reality.

Before he fell so hard for the fairytale he might never recover.

It was good to be back in Copenhagen.

Ellie felt as if she was seeing the city through whole new eyes in Jesper's company. After the week they'd spent mostly in bed in Odense, she'd sort of expected the same once they were back in the city, but life in Copenhagen was very different.

In fact, Jesper had left her at her short-term rental apartment the first night they'd returned, excusing himself to deal with some personal admin. The searing kiss he'd given her on departure, and the fact he'd spent every night since in her bed, meant she hadn't taken it at all personally. And honestly, it had been good to have a little time and space to catch up with herself and her feelings.

It had meant another awkward conversation with her mother, though. This time, at least she'd been rather more confident in her answers.

'Mum, I'm not coming home for the wedding. I'm doing something that is important to me here in Denmark, and I'm not willing to give it up just so Maisie can feel better about marrying my ex-husband.' There had been a sharp intake of breath from her mother there, but Ellie had ploughed on. 'In fact, I can't think of anything more awful for everyone than for them to have the ex-wife there haunting the proceedings at the back of the church. They've moved on and are starting a new life together. Please, let me do the same.'

She'd hung up the phone before her mum could respond, and had poured herself a large glass of white wine to celebrate.

Since then, she'd focused on really making the most of her remaining time in Denmark—and with Jesper. And if she'd expected to be doing that mostly in bed, she'd been wrong. It turned out that Jesper had a long list of places to take her and things to show her and he was determined to get through all of them before she left.

'I made you a promise,' he told her when she questioned the manic schedule. 'I promised to show you exactly why the Danes are so happy, and I intend to fulfil that. I showed you the places that saved me, when I was at my worst. Now I'm showing you all the everyday things that affect the Danish sense of wellbeing. We lost time in Odense, but I think we can still make it up.'

'Or I could always change my flight, I suppose.' The idea wasn't as unattractive as it would have been before New Year. Then, she was just waiting for the wedding to be over so she could go back home. Now…a few more weeks in Denmark with Jesper definitely wouldn't be the worst outcome. Especially since the book was actually coming together, and she wasn't panicking about having to pay back her advance.

But Jesper just gave her a small smile and said, 'Don't worry. We'll get through everywhere on my list in time.'

And so the days passed in a whirlwind of galleries and museums and restaurants and open spaces. Jesper talked to her about the power of architecture and design to affect people's moods, even introducing her to his ex-brother-in-law's husband, who was a designer and spoke about the magic of design with such alacrity that Ellie couldn't help but be inspired. She scribbled notes as fast as she could, and ignored Jesper all evening while she added a new section to the book afterwards.

He took her to a local ceramics centre, where he'd arranged for her to try her hand at pottery-making. As she fashioned an almost serviceable bowl on the wheel—after a few failed early attempts that required Jesper to leave the room so he didn't laugh in her face—they talked about the importance of making things that lasted. How it provided a satisfaction that lasted much longer than fleeting happiness.

'Legacy,' Jesper said, as she focused on her bowl spinning slowly under her hands. 'Like your book. You're creating something that will outlive you, be read by people you'll never meet, live in the world completely apart from you. That's amazing.'

'Unlike this bowl.' Ellie squinted at it. 'I don't think anyone but me will ever want this thing.'

He smiled. 'I would.'

'Then it's yours,' she promised. 'Something to remember me by.'

'I'd like that,' Jesper replied.

But long after the clay had—finally—been cleaned from her hands, and Jesper had arranged to come and collect the bowl after it had been fired, she was still thinking about his words. Was that really what she was trying to do with her book? Outlive herself? She supposed that maybe it was. A way to leave a mark on the world.

She liked that. Almost as much as the thought that Jesper would remember her when she was gone too, every time he looked at that ridiculous, lopsided bowl on his shelf.

After a week of exploring Copenhagen with Jesper, they caught up with Lily and Anders for dinner at Lily's favourite restaurant.

'How are we supposed to act in front of them?'

Ellie asked Jesper in the car on their way over. 'I mean, are we just friends, or do we let them know about...'

'All the sex?' Jesper answered, in his usual, blunt way. 'It's up to you.'

She considered. 'If we tell Lily we're sleeping together, she's going to make it into some personal victory—especially after New Year. Worse, she might decide we're madly in love and I'm moving to Denmark permanently, because that's what she did with Anders. Which is obviously ridiculous.'

The idea of it, though, prickled under her skin. She *wasn't* in love, because that wasn't what she was here in Denmark for. It wasn't the deal. And she definitely wasn't falling in love with a man who had been very clear about not being able to love her back. That way disappointment lay, and she'd had enough of that already lately, thank you.

Jesper shrugged. 'So we just act like friends. How hard can that be?'

It turned out, rather harder than Ellie had anticipated.

She'd thought they were doing a good job of just being friends, until Lily dragged her to the bathroom after the first course and demanded to know what was going on between her and Jesper.

Ellie blinked, and caught her reflection in the mirror, looking like a deer in the headlights. 'I…what do you mean?'

Lily rolled her eyes. 'The pair of you are ridiculous. I mean, the way he smiles at you, the way he handed you your menu, the way he guessed your wine order…not to mention the way he kept brushing his arm against yours. You're clearly sleeping together, and I want to know all the juicy details!'

Ellie glanced down at the bathroom tiles to hide her smile. 'Okay, fine. But later, okay? I want to get back out there before the main course arrives and Jesper starts stealing my sides. He's terrible for sharing food.'

She brushed a hand against the back of Jesper's shoulders as she went to sit down, and let him take her hand and kiss it, and that was the cat completely out of the bag.

They went back to Lily and Anders' flat after dinner, to the scene of their first kiss, and Ellie couldn't help but lose herself in reminiscences as she sank into the squashy sofa. Anders and Jesper were out on the tiny balcony, looking at something in the night sky—Ellie wasn't sure what—so it was just her and Lily now.

Her friend, sitting on the other end of the sofa, studied her carefully, a small frown line forming between her eyebrows.

'You look different.'

Ellie looked up in surprise. 'I stopped dyeing my hair weeks and weeks ago. Last year even, technically. Has it really taken you this long to notice?'

'It's not your hair.' Lily waved a dismissive hand. 'It's your...you. You look, well, happy. Sort of.'

Sort of?

'I *am* happy,' Ellie said. 'Or content, at least.'

'Because of Jesper?' There was a hint of concern in Lily's voice now, and Ellie realised what the problem was. Her friend thought she'd fallen in love with Jesper and was going to get her heart broken.

She shook her head. 'Not the way you mean. He's been...it's all been great. He's been such a huge help with the book, with helping me to see the world, and my future, differently. And now... I finally feel like I'm ready to get back to my real life again, back in London. You know?'

'That's great.' Despite her words, Lily still sounded doubtful. 'But are you sure—'

'You do realise that you're the one who set

the two of us up for New Year, right?' Ellie interrupted.

Lily flushed pink. 'I know. And you haven't even said thank you for that yet, you realise? But I only did it because...'

'Because?' Ellie prompted when she trailed off, genuinely unsure where her best friend was going with this.

'Because I wanted you to have a little fun, and God knows Jesper needed some too, and I thought the two of you would get along well,' Lily said. 'But I didn't imagine... I see the way you look at him, El. And the way he looks at you, for that matter. It's just been so fast! And it's not just a bit of fun any more, is it? And I don't want you to get hurt, is all. You're both—'

She broke off as the door to the balcony opened and Jesper and Anders came back inside. Ellie thought it was probably for the best. She wasn't sure she wanted to hear what Lily had been about to say. It certainly wasn't the reaction she'd expected from her best friend.

'So, where are you two off to next on your Danish magical mystery tour?' Anders was asking.

Jesper shot Ellie an amused look. 'I'm taking her to Hamlet's castle.'

'Kronborg Castle? Brilliant!' Anders grinned at Ellie. 'You'll love it.'

Ellie wasn't so sure. 'I studied Hamlet at A Level. Seems to me there was a lot of waffling and then everybody died.'

'That's pretty much it,' Anders agreed happily. 'But the castle is spectacular.'

'So, "to be or not to be" happy. That's tomorrow's question, then?' Lily got up and tucked herself into Anders' arms as Jesper came and joined Ellie on the sofa in her place.

'Something like that,' he said softly. But there was something in his gaze Ellie couldn't quite place.

She blinked, and it was gone. Probably she'd imagined the strange look.

She hoped so. Because she didn't think she'd ever seen him look so sad. And she couldn't for the life of her figure out why.

CHAPTER TEN

ELLIE HADN'T TOLD him exactly when the wedding day was, only that she was avoiding it by being in Denmark. But she didn't have to. Jesper knew from the moment he woke up in bed alone on the thirty-first of January, the day after they'd visited Hamlet's castle, that it was the day that Ellie's ex-husband would be marrying her half-sister.

Every other morning they'd woken up together, Ellie had been curled up against his side, warm and soft and wonderful. Today, he could hear the clatter of her keyboard in the next room as she wrote.

Normally, she was a late at night writer, often writing until he coaxed her into joining him in bed. He didn't mind; he was happy to read while she worked, and it meant she tended to sleep in with him too, which provided all sorts of opportunities, in his experience.

He'd never seen her get up early to write before. Which was how he knew something must be wrong.

Tugging on some pants and a T-shirt, he checked his phone on the bedside table and saw a text from Lily, warning him that Ellie might need a little extra care and attention that day.

I don't know how much she's told you, but there's something happening in London today that's going to be pretty hard for her. Just look after her for me, okay?

Jesper thought he could do that.

He padded through to the living area of the tiny apartment Ellie had rented in Copenhagen. When they'd returned, he'd considered moving them both to one of his preferred hotels, or even renting a better apartment. He needed to buy somewhere eventually, but there wasn't time for that before she left, no matter how much money he threw at the problem.

But then it had occurred to him that it might be good for them to have their own space in the city. The time when Ellie would have to leave was drawing ever closer, and he knew he needed to start putting some distance between them, to protect himself when the time came. So, their first night back he'd checked into a hotel and forced himself to stay there all night, under the guise of catching up on some admin stuff. In truth, he'd spent the whole night watching bad movies and wishing he was with Ellie.

The next night he'd ended up staying with her in that tiny apartment, and somehow he'd never left again since.

Now, he was glad of it. It meant he was there today, when she needed him.

This day, her ex's wedding day, was the whole reason she'd come to Denmark in the first place. The reason for her happiness quest.

The least he could do was live through it with her, and be there for support.

Jesper leaned against the small kitchen island that separated the living space from the cooking, and watched her. Ellie sat at the small bistro table in the window, still wearing her pyjamas, looking out over the street below, her laptop in front of her, a frown on her face as she typed. A small piece of hair, shining in the weak winter sunlight, kept falling into her eyes. Every few moments she'd brush it away but it would fall straight back again.

God, he loved her. He didn't want her to leave. He wanted to spare her the pain of this day.

But all of that was about him, and none of it was about her.

So he didn't say any of it.

Instead, he eased himself into the chair opposite her, and waited for her to finish her train of thought. After a few more moments of frantic typing, she looked up and smiled.

It looked fragile, he thought. The sort of smile a person put on when they were trying to convince someone else—or themselves—that everything was fine. The sort of smile it made his heart hurt to see on Ellie's beautiful face.

'Hey. Sorry, I just woke up and… I couldn't sleep any more, and then I had an idea about something I needed to include in the book, so I thought I'd get some work done,' she said.

'Makes sense,' he replied. 'You must be hungry by now though. Can you take a break for some breakfast? I could go out and get something, or we could head down to the bakery for pastries.'

She tilted her head to one side, considering. 'You know what? Pastries would be good. Just let me get showered and dressed and we'll go.'

They'd visited a lot of cafés, bakeries and restaurants since they'd been back in Copenhagen, but as they left the apartment Jesper had a hankering for the one where they'd met, back at the start of January, to discuss the trip that became their happiness quest. Ellie looked amused when she realised where they were heading.

'Finally, the truth comes out. The true reason Danes are happier is because of the pastries. You could have just told me that the first day we met here and saved me a lot of time, you know.' She pushed the door open and stepped inside ahead of him, leaving a waft of sugary scent to hit him in the face.

He inhaled, and followed. 'Would you really have wanted that?'

She turned back to face him, a soft smile on her face. 'Not for a moment.'

'Good.'

They ordered a selection of pastries and large coffees before settling in at their table. Jesper tried to keep the conversation light and inconsequential, not wanting to demand too much of her on a day when her mind was clearly elsewhere. But when the coffee was done, neither of them was quite ready to return to the apartment yet.

'We should take a walk,' Jesper suggested. Walking always helped him stay in the moment, rather than obsessing about things he couldn't change, and he suspected that was what she needed today. 'It's a lovely day out there. Well, for January.'

She laughed, and it gladdened his heart to hear it. 'It is. Bright and cold and crisp.' Her face started to fall, and he knew without asking that she was wondering if the weather was the same in London.

He took her arm and got them moving. 'I haven't even taken you to see the Little Mermaid statue yet. I think that might be an actual crime, to come to Copenhagen and not see it.'

She gave him a wan smile. 'Didn't you check out my social media? I walked up the river to see it my first week in Denmark.'

Of course she had. If the Little Mermaid had any message at all, it had to be about fighting for happiness whatever the odds.

'Well, you haven't seen it with me,' he pointed out. 'And maybe you'll see it differently after our visit to the Hans Christian Andersen Museum.'

'Perhaps.' She didn't sound convinced, but she went along with him all the same.

They made their way through the city, past the green domed roof of the marble church, past the familiar buildings of the city, and Jesper realised he wasn't even paying attention to his surroundings because there was a question he needed to ask—one that had been bothering him since before they'd left the apartment.

'So, what was the idea for the book that couldn't wait? What were you working on this morning?'

Ellie stared out into the distance, at the Kastellet, the star fortress, and the river up ahead. They'd walked further than he'd thought already, both lost in their own thoughts. 'I was thinking about something else you need for happiness. Trust.'

'Trust?' Jesper frowned. He hadn't known what to expect, but it hadn't been that.

'Yeah. I figured that happiness is all about trust, really. You have to trust that life will be good, or that things will get better. You have to have faith in life, I suppose. And…and you have to trust other people, too. Or want to trust them at least. Because if you walk around expecting the worst of people all the time, how can you ever be happy?'

'That makes sense, I guess.' And it did. Too much sense. Her words were cascading around his head like a waterfall, and he hated it.

'It's like marriage,' she went on. 'When you get married, you put your whole heart in someone else's hands and trust them not to squeeze too hard.'

Was that what he'd done to Agnes? Taken her heart and squeezed the life out of it?

Was that why she'd left?

Maybe.

But he couldn't think about that now. He had to keep listening, trying to understand what Ellie was saying. 'And once someone has crushed your heart like that…it's hard to imagine trusting anyone that way again. But you have to—you have to trust the world, and you have to trust other people, or how can you be happy? Does that make sense?'

'I… I think so.' It was hard to get the words out. Because right now it felt as if it was *his* heart being crushed. He knew it wasn't because he couldn't trust her, though. But because he couldn't let her trust *him*.

Not when he couldn't trust himself.

Ellie's heart was beating too fast, and she knew it wasn't the cold, bracing air or the leisurely speed of their walk past the red walls of the Kastellet towards the river. She'd done this walk before, and while the sights still enchanted her, they weren't enough to distract her from her own thoughts. Not today.

Up ahead, she saw a small crowd around where she knew the statue of the Little Mermaid sat in the water. Everyone always said it was smaller than they'd imagined, but Ellie liked that about it. Liked the idea of this one, small mermaid taking on forces greater than herself in the pursuit of a life that would make her truly happy.

Of course, she had to admit to preferring Disney's ending to the fairytale than Andersen's.

The crowds parted and she came into view, a small bronze mermaid perched on a rock, staring out into the distance, imagining the life she could have. Did she know even then that she'd give up her voice for human legs, one freedom for another?

Ellie didn't want to give up anything. She wanted it all.

That was the problem.

She knew what she needed to say, but right until the last moment she knew she wouldn't be sure that she'd have the confidence. Instead, she stared at the statue for long seconds, until another crowd of winter tourists came along, and she stepped back to let them see.

Jesper tugged her arm and led her to a nearby bench, where they could still see the statue in between the waxing and waning crowds.

'It's Dave and Maisie's wedding today,' she

said after a moment. It was the first time she'd acknowledged it out loud, even though the fact had been at the front of her mind all day.

'I know,' Jesper said.

'How? Did Lily tell you?' Had he known all morning and not said anything? Why?

He sighed. 'She texted me, yes. But I didn't need her to tell me. I knew the moment I woke up and you weren't in bed with me. But I wasn't sure if you *wanted* me to know, so…'

'So you took me for pastries instead.'

'Basically.' He gave her a small smile and a shrug. 'Was that the wrong thing to do?'

'No. It was…pastries are always good.'

'That was what I thought.' He settled back onto the bench, arms folded over his chest, a pleased smile on his face.

She hoped the smile would stay past what she had to say next.

'It got me thinking, though. The wedding, not the pastries,' she clarified. 'About trust, like I said. But also…about wanting what you can't have, or wanting something and regretting it when you get it. For the longest time, all I wanted was my old life back—my marriage, my friends, the future I'd imagined for us. But now… I wouldn't have it all back as a gift, and I wonder if Maisie will feel that way some day. If she'll realise that my life wasn't what she really wanted at all, and leave Dave in the same state I was in.'

'It's not your responsibility to worry about that for them,' Jesper said softly.

'I know. I know that, I do.' She searched for the right words to explain. 'It's just… I look back at the woman—girl, practically—I was then, when I got married, and I realise that she knew nothing about who she really was, who she could be. I'm not sure I ever did, before now. I just went along doing the next thing and the next thing and never stopping to think if they were really the things that I wanted to be doing in the first place. And then, when it all fell apart, I just ran away. All the way to Denmark.'

'And I, for one, am glad that you did.' He nudged her with his shoulder and she looked up at him and tried to smile.

Because this was the scariest part of all. The part that came next.

'I thought I was running away.' Her throat was dry, and she forced herself to swallow, to keep the words coming. 'But now I wonder if I wasn't running towards something. Towards trusting in happiness again. Towards love. Towards you.'

She wished she wasn't looking at him as she said it. Wished she'd kept her gaze fixed on that hopeful bronze mermaid out in the water, looking towards a better life.

Because if she had been, she wouldn't have had to watch the horror settle over Jesper's face as he realised she'd said the word 'love'.

Love.

She hadn't really said it. Or if she had, she didn't mean it.

This was all because her ex was getting married today. She was maudlin or wistful or something. She was romanticising the life she'd had, and imagining the life she wanted— fantasising that maybe he could give it to her. But he knew that he couldn't—and any other day, he was sure she'd know that too. She wouldn't want him if she wasn't feeling the way she was because of her ex-husband getting remarried.

He'd *told* her—explained how he couldn't be a good enough husband to make Agnes stay. How he always went too far, wanted too much, and couldn't live up to the man people wanted him to be.

She was a people pleaser, keeping the peace and giving others what they needed. If he let her love him, how long would she go along with what he wanted, pretending it was what she wanted too, before it became too much?

Before she left him, the same way Agnes had, because he'd let her down?

So, no. She couldn't mean it.

Because if she meant it, then he would have to be the strong one and walk away. To save them both.

He needed to show her that she couldn't love him. Remind her of everything she'd told him about the importance of her own happiness, and how she didn't want to be dependent on someone else for it.

She hadn't really said the words yet, she hadn't said 'I love you,' even though her eyes were screaming it.

Even though every part of him wanted to say it back.

He broke away to look out across the water. He just needed a moment. He needed to think. He needed to convince her that this was the wrong thing for them. That in the end he'd only ruin it, ruin her. That everything he'd given her the last four weeks was all he could *ever* give her.

And then he needed to walk away.

'You were right, back at the start, when you

told me you couldn't let your happiness be dependent on another person.'

'That's not what I'm doing!' Ellie shot back. 'I lo—'

He couldn't let her say it, so he broke in before she could finish.

'You know... I told you about my marriage. About why I can't do that again. And I'm sorry if I gave you the impression...' Jesper shook his head, words beginning to fail him as the hope started to drain from her face. 'For a short time, I made you my new project, my new obsession. That's what I do, you see? I fall in too deep, too fast, and I obsess and then...it all falls apart.' He looked away, unable to bear the pain in her eyes any more. Instead, he stared out at the river, the ever-changing water, and tried to find some of the peace he'd felt in his three years away from society. 'It took me such a long time to move past Agnes' death. I gave it all up—the business, the New York penthouse, the lifestyle. I handed all my money and investments over to Will, had him sell the company, and trusted him to keep me solvent. I bought the beach house and I just...retreated. I thought I was returning to the way of life Agnes wanted me to have, by being the polar opposite of how

I'd been the last few years of our marriage. But I realise now that I'd just taken things to another extreme. Because that's what I do. And I can't... I can't live that way any more. I have to find a way to have that balance everyone talks about.'

I can't love you. I'll fail again and you'll leave me, and I won't survive that a second time.

'Balance.' Ellie huffed a small laugh. 'That perfect Danish way of living I'm supposed to be writing about. The happy hygge life. *That's* what you're searching for?'

'I don't know. Maybe?' He ran a hand through his hair. 'I just know I can't go on the way I have been. It's too much. It...it doesn't matter how I feel about you, Ellie. Because I'm not ready for it, not yet. I thought I'd moved on, but being with you has only shown me how much I'm still the same man I was back then. Because you're going to leave—if not now, one day, because I can't be what you need. And if I let myself think about what we could have, and what I'll lose, it'll break me again.'

He risked a look back at her face to see if she understood, and was only slightly surprised to find her eyes blazing with anger.

'You've already played our whole story out

to the end without me, haven't you?' she said. 'It's not that you don't care about me, it's that you don't trust yourself, let alone happiness. You won't take the risk that this could be wonderful. Happiness is trust and it's risk too. You have to take a leap of faith, and you won't.'

'I *can't*.' Not again. Not when he'd only so narrowly survived the last time.

Maybe she heard the pain in his voice, or maybe she'd just given up on him, Jesper wasn't sure. But the anger faded from her expression and her shoulders sagged against the back of the bench. 'You were supposed to be my teacher. The one who showed me how to be happy. And you *did*. It just turned out that, in the end, I know more about happiness than you do. Or I'm more willing to take a chance on it, anyway. I'll be happy with or without you, Jesper. I would just rather it was with you.'

'I'm sorry, Ellie.' He wanted to hold her, to kiss her, to do anything to make this better.

Anything except open his whole heart to her and admit how much he loved her.

Because if he did that, he knew he'd never be able to walk away, and the whole terrible cycle would begin again.

So instead, he got to his feet, cast one last

look back at her beautiful face, then turned and walked away, his heart breaking a little more with every step.

CHAPTER ELEVEN

ELLIE STAYED WITH the Little Mermaid, thinking about everything that had happened since she'd arrived in Denmark, or since New Year at least, for a long time. How could it have only been one month since that midnight kiss with Jesper with the fireworks in the background? She felt like a completely different person to the woman who'd gone to the Tivoli Gardens that night.

But at the same time she felt more herself than she had in decades, and she knew that was thanks to Jesper. And while her heart was aching now, she also knew that he'd given her the tools she needed to recover from that heartbreak. To make her new life, shape it the way she wanted.

First, though, she had a book to finish.

She wiped the freezing tears from her face, stood up to say a silent goodbye to the Little Mermaid and headed back to her flat, a new determination in her step.

It took a steely resolve to ignore all the signs of Jesper still lingering in the flat—from the rumpled sheets to an abandoned jumper on the arm of the sofa to other, more personal memories of what they'd done together there—but Ellie was focused. She settled back down in front of her laptop at the bistro table she'd been working at that morning and started reading through everything she'd already written.

By the time she got to the end the sun was going down, and she had a notebook full of scrawled thoughts and observations about the book so far—and how she now knew she needed to write it.

She turned to the next blank page in her notebook and started a new list, mumbling to herself as she worked.

'The structure needs to change, that's obvious. And I want to make more of the vignettes from the places we went, the importance of light and shade, balance…and then the ending…'

Oh, she had big ideas for the ending.

Because, finally, she knew how her Danish adventure ended. With heartbreak, yes, but also with hope.

And that was the story she was going to write.

Starting now.

* * *

The beach house seemed empty without Ellie.

It had never seemed empty before. It had always *been* empty, he supposed, apart from him. But it had never *felt* that way until now. Before, it had always been a retreat, a place to rest and restore and regroup. It didn't need anyone else in it.

Now...

Well. Lots of things were different now.

Or maybe that was just the vodka talking.

He took another sip as he stared out of the window, watching the moon reflecting on the water, breaking and reforming with every wave. This was the same window seat Ellie had sat in so often during her visit, reading, writing notes in her notebook or even typing away, while he cooked in the kitchen, usually.

He felt closer to her here. Which was ridiculous because she was still miles away in Copenhagen.

If she hadn't gone back to London already. She was supposed to leave in two days' time, but what if she'd changed her ticket? Would Lily have told him if she had?

Lily and Anders hadn't been in touch at all since he'd left Ellie at the Little Mermaid a week before, so he didn't know. Didn't even know if Ellie had told them about their...was it a breakup? He wasn't even sure what to call it if they'd never really been a couple. Just two people travelling the same path for a while. And now they weren't.

And now Jesper couldn't sleep.

Partly it was because he missed her warmth at his side, burrowing in to keep warm, or just stay close.

And partly it was because every time he closed his eyes he relived every moment of his life where he'd screwed up. Where he could have done better. Where he didn't see the problems until it was too late. It wasn't even just Agnes and Ellie. It was every single mistake he'd made since his memories started, before he'd even gone to school.

Maybe his brain was trying to make him learn something from them. But if so, he had no idea what.

With a sigh, he sank down onto the window seat, pretending to himself for a moment that he could still smell Ellie's perfume there. He rested his head against the window and watched the waves for a moment, glass of vodka still in hand.

He supposed that every mistake he'd made had led him here. And so had every right choice, too. For all the things that had gone wrong, it was hard to regret many of the things that he'd done or chosen in his life. Despite how it ended, his marriage to Agnes had been a blessing, and so had his work in New York. Would he do things differently now, knowing what he knew?

He'd try to. He'd try harder. He supposed that would have to be enough.

Or would it? Ellie's words floated back to him.

'She wanted you to earn a lot of money but resented the time it took. She didn't like the trade-off.'

Jesper remembered his own response, repeated it to the empty room. 'I just wasn't good enough. I couldn't give her what she needed.'

I don't think anybody could.

Was she right?

Maybe there had been a way to save their marriage, to find a life they were both satisfied with, happy even. But maybe, just maybe, it wouldn't have only been him who had to change. In another world, perhaps they could have found a compromise. If the car hadn't crashed...

He'd never know for sure. But suddenly it seemed possible that he wasn't the only person in that marriage who'd been at fault. And while he'd always mourn the death of his wife, he couldn't change it. Nothing he did now would change the facts of that terrible afternoon.

He was living in a different world now. A post-Agnes world.

And that was where he'd met Ellie. He wouldn't change that either, now.

But he'd made his choices, and they'd brought him here. Alone, with his vodka and the moon.

And this was where he'd always be, he realised suddenly. Because if he wanted that perfect balance, to maintain a cool, calm life with no space for the extremes that had led him into trouble so often before…well, there was no room for other people in that life. On the periphery, perhaps, looking on and checking in, before they went back to their own fuller, happier lives.

He'd thought he could work past what had happened with Agnes, but being with Ellie had only shown him that he was still the same person he'd always been.

Perhaps he always would be.

So maybe he just needed to accept that person and find a way to live with him. To make it work.

And he had to decide now if he really wanted to do that alone, for ever.

He stood up suddenly, his mind racing to keep up with his thoughts, and dislodged a cushion from the window seat, sending a piece of paper fluttering to the ground. With a frown he picked it up and read it.

Ellie's looping writing filled the page.

Happy Things she'd titled it. And below was a list of things that must have been making her happy in that moment. And they were all…tiny. Inconsequential.

> *Jesper's coffee machine.*
> *The birds on the water outside the window.*
> *The quiet here.*
> *The way he looks at me sometimes.*
> *Pastries for breakfast.*
> *Knowing it's almost time for our next adventure. The troll Jesper bought me at the museum, and its ridiculous red hair.*

None of them were earth-changing. But as he read them, Jesper found himself smiling.

And suddenly something clicked inside his head, almost like a switch, a lightbulb turning on.

Happiness didn't have to be that extreme he'd always thought. It wasn't all or nothing, burn out or checking out, New York City or three years in the wilderness.

It could be those small moments in a long day. An appreciation of the world around him—and the people around him, too. The comforting presence of someone he loved, even when they weren't saying anything...

And he did love Ellie. He'd accepted that much, and it was far too late to stop the feeling now. He'd thought it would lead him—or worse, her—to another ruin.

But maybe...maybe he could just love her in small, everyday ways. And he could do that well enough that they could find happiness, a future together.

If he could even convince her to give him another chance to try.

Jesper put down his drink, folded Ellie's happiness list and tucked it in his pocket and headed to his room to pull out his suitcase.

He had things to arrange.

It was done. The book was done, and Ellie could hardly believe it.

She wasn't sure she'd left the chair for the last week, except to pass out in bed, use the bathroom or acquire food, but the book was done.

And it was good.

She stretched her arms high above her head, feeling something pop in a strangely pleasurable way, then read back over her last few paragraphs one last time before sending it to her agent for her thoughts.

Happiness can be so many things to so many people. We think the Danes have it nailed, and they do, in their own way. So many things about their lifestyle are conducive to also having the time, freedom, space and money to seek out joy in the world.

But one thing I discovered in the long Danish winter was that happiness can so often only be really seen in the contrasts. When night falls before we're ready, we have to trust that the sun will rise again in the morning. That when life seems dark, the brightness of happiness may be only just around the corner, if we can keep our faith in it long enough to find it.

In the end, permanent joy, the 'happiness' I think so many of us are seeking, is an impossibility—simply because, without the contrasts, we soon fail to appreciate what we have. Better, I've found, to strive instead for a resilient sense of personal joy. One that finds bright moments in dark days—but also acknowledges and works through that darkness, ready to step back into the light when we're ready.

The world is full of happy, joyous things— and also sad and humbling, hurtful ones. We have to learn to live a life between the two, finding our balance on life's tightrope, and turning our face towards the sun whenever we get the chance.

In short: happiness is made, not found. We just have to look for it, recognise and enjoy it when it comes, and trust that, when it seems far away, it will return, just like the sun.

Ellie sat back with a satisfied sigh. She'd need to edit it more, she knew—and she was certain that both her agent and her editor would have changes they wanted made, clarifications and explanations, not to mention tidying up her writing.

But she thought that she'd finally found what she'd come to Denmark to write. She'd never expected to write it so fast, but a looming deadline and a little heartbreak did wonders for her writing process, it seemed.

She quickly attached the manuscript to an email before she could have any second thoughts, and sent it off to her agent before closing her laptop down.

She was done. And that meant it was time to go home.

Her flight was booked for late the following afternoon, but tonight she had one last night in Copenhagen with Lily and Anders to enjoy.

She spent an hour or so packing up her belongings, wondering how she had so many more than she'd arrived in the country with— from hygge candles and blankets from Lily when she'd seen the bare furniture of the flat she'd rented, to the troll with the red hair that she still couldn't look at too long without crying. When she'd done as much as she could for now, she hopped in the shower and made herself look presentable for her last night on the town.

The book was done, her trip was over.

It was time to go home and start her new life.

'You're here!' Lily greeted Ellie with a huge hug when she arrived at their apartment later that evening. 'Did you see the lights on the way? They're even better in the city centre. Come on in!'

They'd made plans, early in Ellie's visit, to do a tour of the Copenhagen Light Festival on her last night in Denmark. And however much Ellie hadn't felt like it a week ago when Lily had reminded her about the date, there was no way she was going to be allowed to get out of it. Now the day had arrived, Ellie was glad that Lily hadn't let her cancel. It was good to mark the end of this period of her life with something tangible. Plus, she hoped it would give her one last happy memory of Denmark for the road.

They shared a delicious dinner at the apartment before venturing out, during which nobody mentioned Jesper, which Ellie appreciated. She'd given her friend a bare bones account of what had happened, but hadn't mentioned the part about love. She knew Lily wouldn't let her leave if she thought there was a chance that Jesper could be persuaded to rethink—but Lily hadn't seen his face before he'd walked away.

This was the right decision, for both of them. Ellie had no plans to chase after a man who had made it so clear he didn't want what she had to offer.

Lily *did* ask about the wedding, however.

'Have you spoken to your mum? How did it all go? Was the church struck by lightning when Dave said his vows?'

Ellie chuckled. 'Nothing so dramatic, I'm afraid. Apparently, it all went off without a hitch. I haven't spoken to Mum, but I had a call with Sarah the other day and she filled me in on it all. In fact, she had a message for me from Dave.'

Lily's eyebrows shot up. '*Really?* And what did the devil incarnate have to say?'

'Just that he was sorry Mum and Maisie had been pressuring me to be there—seems he didn't know about it until Sarah mentioned it,' Ellie explained. 'He agreed that it was best I wasn't present, I think. It would have all been just too weird.'

Lily raised her glass. 'Amen to that.'

Once dinner was over, they ventured out onto the streets of Copenhagen to enjoy the light festival. It was, Ellie had to admit, pretty spectacular. Denmark knew how to do light, she reflected, and how to make the most of the light it had. Here, whole buildings were lit up, or had pictures or patterns projected on them, some looking like water, others like rustling leaves. The lights weren't static; they kept moving, illuminating new pockets of the city she'd never seen before, as well as highlighting some of its most famous features. Even the river was lit, with lights strung over boats and beams shooting into the sky. Ellie wondered if they'd make it as far as the Little Mermaid, and what lights she'd have around her tonight.

The streets were crowded with tourists and

locals alike, all taking in the spectacle. For a moment, Ellie felt a pang of sadness; it was so like New Year's Eve it was hard not to compare how each event had ended in her head. One with a kiss, and a new adventure in this country she'd come to love, the other with her leaving for good, alone.

But no. She wasn't going to think about it that way. Because tomorrow was another fresh start, and how lucky was she to have that?

'Oh, look!' Lily grabbed her arm and dragged her across a street. 'The Tivoli Gardens are all lit up too! Let's get closer and see…'

But before they even reached the gates of the Tivoli Gardens, Lily took a sudden turn, down a darkened street. 'Maybe there's something down here.'

Ellie frowned at the map in her hand and glanced back at Anders, who was standing at the entrance to the street, effectively blocking the route. 'There's nothing on the map, Lily. Let's head back to the main street.'

But Lily kept pulling her forward. 'No, I really think there's going to be something to see this way.'

They turned one last corner, into a courtyard Ellie hadn't even known was there. Lily swung her arm so Ellie moved ahead, taking a few small steps to catch her balance. 'What are you—'

She broke off as the lights ahead dazzled her.

This display hadn't been on her official light festival map, she was sure of it. A circle of rainbow lights shone down from the sides of the surrounding buildings, filling the entire courtyard. Red ran into orange then yellow and all the way through to violet, spinning and shifting, like a river of light, always moving. It was huge and bright—and far away from any of the tourists who'd come for the festival. Because this display was only for her.

It was the rainbow panorama at Aarhus recreated just for her. A never-ending circle of light that changed and adapted but kept going all the same.

And standing right in the middle of it, beside a bistro table laden with Danish pastries and a bottle of champagne, was the man who'd first kissed her in that same rainbow.

Ellie glanced behind her and realised Lily had gone—back to join Anders, she assumed. Because, of course, it wasn't the lights Lily had wanted her to see.

Clearly, this was another set-up, just like Lily's plans on New Year's Eve.

Ellie wondered how this one would end.

'Jesper.' His bright blue eyes shone in the lights that scattered across the courtyard. She had no idea how he'd been able to set up such a display, but she knew that he had—just for her.

When she hesitated about whether to step closer or not, Jesper took the decision for her, moving towards her with swift steps, but staying a respectful distance away, just within the rainbow circle. If she wanted to join him, she'd have to cross the swirling colours, turning slowly in from one shade to the next. He wasn't assuming anything. That was good.

Even if every inch of her body was fighting against her head to jump into his arms.

She needed to know what this was, first.

'I'm sorry,' he said. 'For surprising you, and for everything else. I needed to talk to you but I knew you'd have no reason to listen, so I wanted to *do* something, something more than words, and this was my best idea. Lily said... I think she thought this would be romantic.'

'I thought romantic was the last thing you wanted to be with me any more,' she snapped back.

He winced. 'I'm definitely sorry for letting you think that. I just... Can I have a few moments of your time, before you leave for London? I've got champagne. And pastries. And if, when I'm done talking, you never want to see me again, I promise I'll stay away.'

Ellie nodded, ignoring the shudder that went through her middle at the idea of never seeing him again. 'Okay. We can talk.'

She took a breath, waiting for Jesper to move back towards the table in the centre of the courtyard before she approached the rainbow lights shining down. She needed a moment to recalibrate. To try and figure out if this was another ending—or perhaps the fresh start she'd never imagined she could have.

Despite herself, something an awful lot like hope was blooming in her chest.

After all, hadn't she just written that people needed to look out for joy, in order to find it? Something like that anyway.

After a moment, she stepped forward, bracing herself as she reached the light barrier— even though she knew that was ridiculous. The colours were nothing but beams of light, they couldn't stop her, couldn't hurt her. Even if the man in the centre of them could—and already had.

Jesper pulled out a chair for her and she sat, tensed, and stared at the pastries as he took his own seat, then poured her a glass of champagne.

'You know, when we met in that café, back at the start of January, I really did believe that I could teach you about happiness,' Jesper said eventually. 'I thought I'd got it all sorted out. I'd come back from the brink, from the darkest moment, and I thought I was happy. I believed I could share that with you. But instead…' He shook his head. 'Instead, you taught me.'

Her breath caught in her throat. She wanted to say something, but the words seemed trapped. Her heart, though, was beating loudly enough to speak for her anyway.

Jesper put down his glass and reached across the table to rest his open palm on it, ready for her to take, if she chose. But she couldn't, not yet. She needed to hear something more.

'I love you too. That's what I should have said that day, by the Little Mermaid. I love you, and I didn't believe I could ever have that again. But falling in love with you showed me how the life I'd carved out for myself after Agnes' death wasn't happiness. It was existing, simply existing within these strict parameters I'd given myself to keep me in check. To stop me feeling *anything* too much or too fully, in case I lost it or screwed up again and fell back down into that pit. I thought I could protect myself

250 COPENHAGEN ESCAPE WITH THE BILLIONAIRE

from having someone else leave me by choosing to leave first, but I was wrong. You taught me what happiness looks like for me now, and I only realised it when I walked away and felt the pain and the darkness that was left in my life without you.' He took a deep breath, and Ellie realised she was leaning in so close now that she could see the smallest spark of hope in his eyes, and his breath on the air as he spoke again. Her fingers inched towards his. 'So, if you can trust me with your happiness, I'd like to spend the rest of my life loving you, and making you as happy as you make me. If that's still what you want.'

Was it? She'd just got used to the idea of moving on alone, of starting over, taking what she'd learned here and starting again.

But what if she could start again *with him?*

You have to recognise happiness when you see it.

And she was pretty damn sure the tight, bright feeling of joy in her chest was nothing but pure happiness.

Ellie folded her fingers with his on the table, then reached up with her other hand to cup his cheek. Then, in the middle of a rainbow, she leaned across and pressed her frozen lips against his.

* * *

Jesper sank into Ellie's kiss with an overwhelming feeling of relief. He hadn't got a plan B, didn't know what he'd have done if she'd walked away. But he'd had to take the leap of faith, anyway.

Had to trust it would be worth it, if he got to be with her again.

And it was.

Keeping her hand in his, he guided them to their feet and moved around the table to kiss her again—deeper this time. He wrapped his arms around her middle, holding her close and, as she held him back, he vowed to himself that this time, this time he'd never let her go.

Not now he knew what real happiness felt like.

When they finally broke the kiss, Ellie fell back on her heels and looked up at him, a little breathless, he was pleased to note. Maybe she'd even missed him half as much as he'd missed her. The lights from his rainbow circle flickered over her pale skin, highlighting her soft smile, and he felt his chest tighten just to be near her again.

'What changed your mind?' she asked.

Jesper pulled the *Happy Things* list he'd found at the beach house from his pocket and handed it to her. 'I realised that happiness wasn't what I thought it was. And that if I clung onto my old ideas I'd be alone for the rest of my life—worse, I'd be without *you*. I realised you were right—I had to take a risk and trust in happiness. So I came back to see if I could persuade you to give me another chance—a chance for us to be happy together.'

'I'm very glad you did,' she murmured, looking down at her list. Then, with a quick smile, she pulled a pen from the pocket of her coat and added something to the bottom. She turned it around to show him; it read: *Kissing Jesper.*

He laughed, and wrapped his arms tight around her to pull her close again. 'So does that mean you'll stay here in Denmark with me?'

She shook her head. 'I have to go back to London.'

'Right. Of course you do.' Jesper tried not to feel too disappointed. He'd known it wouldn't be that easy.

'But I'll come back.' Ellie grabbed his hand and ducked closer so he was looking into her eyes. 'I'll come back, and you'll come and visit and I'll show you all the things in London that make me believe in happiness, too. And we can decide what happens next, together.'

'Together.' He liked the sound of that.

In fact…maybe *that* was the balance he really needed. Not to stop caring or doing or wanting or loving so much. Just someone else to do it with him. To keep him balanced.

They'd taken the biggest leap of faith together, and now, as the rainbow flickered around them, constantly changing but never ending, Jesper knew one thing for certain.

They'd never stop looking for happiness together.

* * * * *

If you enjoyed this story,
check out these other great reads from
Sophie Pembroke

Christmas Bride's Stand-In Groom
Socialite's Nine-Month Secret
Cinderella in the Spotlight
Best Man with Benefits

All available now!